# Bachelor GRUMP

I0565582

WILLOW FOX and
ALLISON WEST

# ONE

*Elisa*

HIS NAME IS WESTON GRUMP. I kid you not, the man's last name is Grump. It's funny, he does look like a grump. His jaw is always tight and he does seem rather serious when I've run into him in the hallway.

He's the new tenant in our building.

And from what I hear, a bachelor.

There's no ring on his finger, and I've smiled, made polite conversation a handful of times.

And he asked me out for drinks at a bar down the street. To say I'm ecstatic would be an understatement. But I know it's dangerous.

If it doesn't work out, we live in the same building.

Yikes.

He's gorgeous and easy on the eyes, with his thick, dark hair and scruffy beard. Every time I see him, he's always in a suit. He could be a professional male model. But I honestly don't know what he does for a living.

I head to the bar, having agreed to meet him there after work. I'm a little surprised he didn't offer to pick me up, since we're next-door neighbors, but I can't fault the man. Maybe he had plans before our date?

As long as it wasn't another date with someone else first.

But I'm sure he's not like that. Just because he's hot, doesn't mean he hooks up with a random girl every night.

I stalk into the bar, but he's not there. I glance at my watch. I'm two minutes early, not a lot of extra time, but I was running late curling my hair and fixing my makeup.

I grab a seat at the bar, putting my coat on the stool beside me to save Weston a seat. I order a martini and hand over my credit card to open a tab.

Wes hurries into the bar, glancing around. When he locates me, he nods and steps toward the bar counter.

I move my jacket, giving him a place to sit. He gestures to the bartender and orders a rum and Coke. "It's nice to see you again, Elisa." His gaze moves over my dress. "You look very nice."

"Thank you, you don't look so bad yourself," I say with a smirk.

He grabs his glass and takes a swig, offering me a nod. "How long have you lived in our building?"

The way he calls it *our* building sends a warm jolt of lightning through me. I tuck a strand of hair behind my ear. "Three years," I say. "Almost four. What about you? You moved from Denver, is that right?"

He cocks a sly grin. "That is correct, although I don't remember telling you that."

I press my lips together and reach for my martini. The girls in the building talk, especially when it's about a handsome new guy who moved in and he's evidently single. "Word travels fast," I say, and sip my drink. Guilty as charged.

"Gossiping will get you nowhere in life," Weston says. The smile fades from his face as he glances at my drink and then at me. "Have you eaten dinner?"

I shake my head. "I just got off work. Looking forward to a nice long weekend before I have to face my new boss."

He nods but doesn't say anything. Weston takes another swig of his rum and Coke. "We should get some food." He stalks across the bar for an empty booth and waits for me to get up to join him.

"Okay," I say, and climb down from the barstool. I grab my coat and purse, taking everything with me to the booth.

Weston examines the menu while I return back to the bar counter to grab my drink. The waitress is already at the table, taking his order.

"We'd like an order of Philly cheesesteak meatballs, mozzarella sticks, quesadillas, nachos, one pound pretzel, and artichoke and quinoa stuffed mushrooms." The waitress scribbles it all down before rushing off to put the order into the computer.

"That's a lot of food for one person," I say, sliding into the booth and placing my drink on the table. I reach for the menu to look it over.

"I ordered for both of us."

"I can't have dairy," I say. Most of what he ordered would make me sick. Six months ago, I had emergency surgery, and my gallbladder was removed. Since then, I've been plagued with lactose intolerance.

"Then I guess you can have the pretzel."

"Or I can find something on the menu to eat," I say, and open the menu, finding something that looks appetizing. I gesture the waitress over and add an order of wings.

"Anything else?" she asks.

"That's it for me."

Weston stares at his phone, nestled in his hand. He seems more interested in his smartphone than me at the moment. "I'll have a Flaming Dr. Pepper. Do you want another drink?" He doesn't so much as glance up at the waitress.

"I'll have another martini. Thank you," I say as she hurries off to put the rest of our order into the system.

"Everything okay?" I ask.

"Yeah, it's nothing." He shoves his phone into his pocket.

"Work?" I guess.

"Just family stuff." He doesn't elaborate. "You've been in the building three years, you mentioned. I take it you like it?"

"It's nice. I haven't had any issues with any other tenants."

"Good." His eyes wander toward the bar, and I shift uncomfortably as he stares at a blonde with another guy. They're having drinks in the spot we vacated.

"Do you know her?" I ask.

"Who?" Weston gives me the clueless look, but I get the feeling that she might be an ex.

It doesn't matter. "No one." I exhale a sigh and finish the last of my martini, relieved when the waitress brings a second one to the table, just in time.

———

There have been rumors that our boss, the Executive Producer and, more importantly, head of acquisitions was leaving. I'm not sure whether it was willingly or not, but the gossip has been spreading like wildfire.

"Elisa, oh my gosh, you got your hair cut short and I love the new color. It's cute!" Sloane is chipper this morning.

"It looks okay?" I ask, worried that it didn't turn out after the disaster of a date.

"Of course. Why?"

I exhale a breathy laugh. "Well, my next-door neighbor, and hot date, set my hair on fire."

"What? No way!"

I wish I were joking. "Well, it wasn't his fault. The waitress got bumped into when she lit the flame and the next thing I know, my head is slammed against the table and there's a jacket on my face. Utterly romantic and mortifying," I mutter.

"Did you get burned?" Sloane asks, her eyes wide. She glances me over, but she doesn't see any evidence of the fire. That's because there isn't any, except for my hair, which went up in seconds.

"No, thankfully, my date was quick to act and pretty much beat me with his coat."

"Sounds sexy. I'm glad you're okay."

"Thanks, and it really wasn't. It was embarrassing and just awful. I mean, the date went from bad to worse."

"Wait?" Sloane's mouth drops. "That wasn't the worst part?"

"No, it probably was, but he kept eyeing this blonde girl, like he wanted to be with her instead of me." I tug my bottom lip between my teeth. "Bad date."

"Date from hell," Sloane corrects me. "Oh, did you hear that we're getting a new head of acquisitions? Rumor has it that some new bigwig from out west is getting the Executive Producer role and we'll be forced to report to him."

"I saw John clean out his desk on Friday. Have you seen who they hired?" I keep hoping they'll promote someone on our team.

"I caught a glimpse of him when he met with HR this morning, and let me tell you, girl, he's eye candy." Sloane's cheeks are red as she fans her face.

"Yeah? When do we meet him?" Not that I'm excited to gain a new boss, but reporting to the CEO has been difficult, since he's never at the office. He works at a different location, and our Executive Producer typically had direct contact with the CEO.

"You get to meet him now," a deep voice says, and I inhale sharply. "Weston Grump, and don't you dare comment on my last name."

My tongue swipes across my top lip. How long had he been standing out in the hallway? How much had he heard?

"Mr. Grump," I say, and stand, holding out my hand to properly introduce myself. "Elisa Emerson, I'm your acquisitions editor."

"Wonderful," he says, staring at me, locking eyes, and the air seems to be sucked out of the room.

"I'm Sloane Michaels," my colleague says, standing up to introduce herself.

"Nice to meet you, Ms. Michaels," Weston says.

"Just call me Sloane. We're all pretty informal around here."

I'm glad Sloane is talking, because, right now, my mouth is prickly like a cactus. Does Weston recognize me? The last time he saw me on Friday night, my hair was long, blonde, and lit on fire.

After that disaster, I bolted and went home, vowing never to see him again.

On Saturday, I made an emergency appointment at the hairdresser's. I had her fix the disaster, and in the process of cutting, we also did a full color. With my pale skin, I look a bit gothic for my taste, but I don't care. I'm grateful for the change.

Is it possible Weston doesn't know I'm the girl from Friday night? He hasn't let on, other than the long stare. Maybe he thinks I'm familiar? I'll go with that. But it's not like a name like Elisa is all too common.

"Miss Emerson, I suggest you grab a paper and pen. My office. Ten minutes." He turns and heads back toward his private office.

"What do you think he wants?" Sloane asks, wiggling her eyebrows suggestively.

"Stop it," I hiss, glaring at her. I don't have the courage to tell her that *he* was my lousy date. "He's our boss."

"And he's hot as sin. Girl, let me have the fantasy, at least until he starts bossing us all around."

"You know he will," I say. "With a surname like Grump, it's inevitable." I don't tell her how he was an awful date. And while catching my hair on fire wasn't his fault, him constantly ogling the blonde and checking his phone was entirely on him.

I guess he had a thing for blondes. It's a good thing I'm no longer his type.

Sloane's laughter bounces off the open walls. "Girl, get it together." My eyes widen, and I dread that Mr. Grump might come out to see what all the fuss is about. There's no chance we're letting him in on the joke.

Although it kind of feels like the joke is on me, having gone out with him.

Chalk it up to experience and lousy dating apps. You have to kiss a lot of frogs to meet your prince. And Weston Grump is one hundred percent a frog. I mean, he's easy on the eyes, has a gorgeous body, and that smile, when he offers it, makes my heart strum, and I get those tingly flutters that make me flush. But he's still a grump.

I grab a pen from my desk and a blank notepad to jot down whatever Mr. Grump wants to discuss. I head for his office and give a firm knock before entering.

"Come in," he says, and I step into his office. "Shut the door behind you."

I inhale a nervous breath and try not to let him see my hand tremble. "You wanted to see me, Mr. Grump."

"Call me Weston." He glances up from his desk, not amused. "Take a seat." He gestures to the empty chair across from his desk.

"Yes, sir." I follow his instructions. It's not that big of a deal, him having me sit in his office. I'm sure that I'll have to work with him quite a bit if I'm going to be working under him. Unless he realizes that he hates it here, and there's a chance he'll move on, go and work someplace else?

"How long have you been with the company, Miss Emerson?" he asks, respecting my request to be addressed by my last name.

"Seven years, sir."

"And in that time, have you ever met the CEO?"

I inhale sharply. "No." My brow tightens. What is this line of questioning about?

"Pen. Paper?"

"Right here," I say, tapping my uncapped pen against the blank slate. "Do you have a meeting, sir? You mentioned that I would need to take notes."

"That was an assumption that you made, taking notes. I need you to draft a proposal that will be going out company-wide and then to our PR department."

"Okay," I say, unsure what I'll be writing.

"The CEO of Blazing Media, my father, passed away last night. I have taken over the company as per the terms of his last will and testament—" Weston stares at me. "Why aren't you writing?"

"Oh, right. Sorry, Mr. Grump." I jot down the information that Weston provides me with, which isn't very much.

"With the passing of my father and his absence from the media house, I am the new CEO." His eyes narrow. "Scratch that. Put something like, in this unforeseen circumstance, Mr. Weston Grump has been appointed the new CEO. While there will be changes in the coming future, everyone can rest assured that Blazing Media will continue to produce romance films for the foreseeable future."

I jot down as much as I can, but my wrist cramps, and Mr. Grump doesn't seem to notice.

"I'm sorry for the loss of your father," I say.

"Save it, Miss Emerson. Your sucking up won't do you a lick of good around here." There's a harshness that resonates with him, but I want to believe it's because he's grieving, and his father just passed away unexpectedly. "I need a draft of that typed out and on my desk within the hour."

It's not a question. "Of course, I will get right on that," I say.

He stares at me. "You're dismissed."

My jaw drops. "I have a question for you, Mr. Grump."

His nostrils flare. "I hope you take direction better when you write, because your listening skills are significantly lacking. It's Weston. Call me Weston." His jaw is clenched as he glares at me. When he realizes that I'm not leaving his office, he gestures to speak. "Go on."

"Will you be hiring a replacement for the Executive Producer position? Sloane and I thought that you were the new hire this morning," I say, putting the cap back on my pen.

"No, we will be under a hiring freeze for the next several months while I examine the books and our profitability to see what is and isn't working around here. My father, technically stepfather, wasn't very hands-on with the company. I intend to change that moving forward."

Mr. Grump stands and heads to the office door, opening it.

"You will be reporting directly to me, Miss Emerson. I expect that letter on my desk in fifty-five minutes."

"Yes, sir."

I hurry out of his office and back to my desk. In a matter of minutes, I'm tapping away at the keyboard.

"So, any gossip?" Sloane asks.

"He wants me to draft a company-wide memo," I say.

"Anything juicy?"

"I'll give you one hint; he's not the Executive Producer."

Her eyes widen. "Savage. Who is he? What's his role?"

I click away at the keys on the computer, trying my damnedest to get the memo finished ahead of schedule. Not like Mr. Grump gave me a lot of time to finish the email.

"You'll have to wait," I say, not ready to spill his secrets. She'll find out when he sends the companywide email to all employees.

Sloane stares at his office like she's envisioning the man naked or something. I swear she's drooling and obsessed with him. "He's hot. Any word on if he's married?"

That would be my luck. The bachelor in apartment 4B isn't actually a bachelor. Wouldn't be the first time that I was duped. But I haven't seen any signs of a wife or girlfriend. No ring for starters, and his office is pretty bare of any pictures. But it's only his first day.

"I don't think he is, but he's off-limits. Trust me," I say without elaborating.

"Obviously, Elisa. He's our boss. But I swear he could be an underwear model."

"Trust me. He's not worth it. The good-looking ones all think they're hot shit. Mr. Grump may be dreamy, but I'm sure that in bed his dick is a little pecker, and he can't even rock the boat. He probably keeps a cucumber in there, so girls think he's got a giant dick, but in reality, it's like one of those mini cucumbers."

A thick, heavy voice clears his throat. "Elisa, my office now!" he snaps at me.

Sloane bursts out laughing, and I throw my pen at her. She dodges the missile, grinning at me like she's proud that I got called to the principal's office.

Fuck.

Am I about to get fired?

I bring my laptop with me, grabbing it from the dock. If Mr. Grump requires that I take more notes, it'll be easier doing so with the laptop.

He lets me step into his office first, and then he slams the door abruptly behind himself.

I inhale sharply, and there's a chill in the air. My arms are covered in goosebumps.

"Do you find it appropriate to talk about my junk to another staff member?"

"I don't know what you're talking about," I say, trying to think up any excuse to escape this new brand of hell I've found myself involved in.

But there's no way out. I did this to myself and I'm going to have to pay for it.

# TWO

*Weston*

I THOUGHT the weekend was bad. I wasn't expecting Monday to be worse. After learning of my stepfather's passing and dealing with the lawyer over the weekend, I show up to Blazing Media first thing Monday morning.

The HR team, at least, was expecting me, but only a handful of people are aware of the situation, that I'm now CEO.

It's not like I don't know the company. I've been working under my stepfather, helping him for the past ten years. The man had some memory issues lately, and I was doing most of his work while he got the credit.

It's why he was never in the office.

And it worked for me for the better part of the last couple of years, working from his home while having a son to look after.

At the moment, my son, three, is in daycare across town, closer to where I used to live. I'm renting a two-bedroom place in a condo complex while my house is undergoing renovations. Changing preschools for Tyler isn't ideal, especially if we will be back in the house around or shortly after Christmas.

Apparently, the old estate had lead paint on the walls and asbestos siding and roofing. Had I known, I'd have done the renovations sooner.

And while I'm not looking forward to moving, even temporarily, because Tyler needs stability in his life, I also don't want to put his health at risk. He's already so fragile.

Tyler means the world to me. Never in my life did I imagine having kids. I sure as hell didn't plan any of it, and I'll do whatever is necessary to keep him safe.

Which usually means casual dating and not bringing a girl home. I rarely tell anyone I'm a father. It doesn't mean I'm not proud of my son. It's just no one's business. Besides, I'm a billionaire. I don't want anyone getting the crazy idea that they can kidnap my boy for ransom.

I've seen the movies. And yes, I have plenty of top-notch security at my house. The condo I'm renting is a different story. So, I have to keep a low profile to protect my boy.

I should also have kept my dick in check when I saw the cute blonde next door.

Instead, I'm the one being tortured by the one bad date that I went on Friday night. How the hell did Elisa catch her hair on fire?

It wasn't the first Flaming Dr. Pepper that I ordered, and maybe that had been the mistake. Not mine, but the waitress had grown too cocky and forgot to blow out the shot before tossing it into the glass of beer.

And just as she did that, some asshat opened a door and brought in just enough wind to whip Elisa's gorgeous blonde locks into the flames.

I don't think I'll ever drink again.

Well, nothing set aflame.

I still can't get that horrifying image from my head, and I blanketed her with my jacket, dowsing the flames as quickly as they took.

Her face and skin were unscathed, but her long locks were singed. Elisa claimed to have to go to the bathroom, but she must have snuck out the back door, because she didn't come back to the table.

What a fucking nightmare.

Oh, and it gets worse. My ex-girlfriend was grabbing drinks at the bar. And it wasn't with her new husband. Just when I thought I was finally over her.

To top off my spectacular Monday, Elisa is an employee of Blazing Media, and I walked in, catching her talking about my cock to one of the staff members.

What the actual hell?

Could my life become any more complicated?

I run a hand through my hair, and I'm trying not to lose my cool, because I'm about to blow a fucking gasket. "Do you make it a habit of talking about your boss's cock to other employees?" I pin her with my stare.

Her pale-blue eyes flutter up at me under her thick dark eyelashes. It's such a stark contrast to her raven hair.

After the fire damaged her hair, she went from having long hair halfway down her back to a short trim above the shoulders. But instead of the blonde, her hair has been dyed jet black. Gothic isn't her color, but I bite my tongue, knowing better than to comment on a woman's hairstyle.

"No, sir," Elisa says. "It was completely out of line."

"Damn straight," I growl. "Did you tell gossipy Sloane about Friday night?"

She bites down on her bottom lip.

Guilty as charged.

Shit.

I exhale a breath. "Do I need to inform HR about what occurred prior to us working together?"

She's quick to shake her head. "No, that isn't necessary. We had one lousy date. We both know that it won't ever happen again."

"Good," I say, glad she's on the same page. I don't appreciate being ditched during a date. Even if I wasn't on my A game, I wasn't the one who lit her hair on fire. She didn't have to run out the back door. I'd have taken her home if she wanted to leave. I can be a gentleman when the moment arises.

She exhales a shaky breath. "Is there anything else? I'm almost done with the draft that you requested." Her laptop is clutched in her hands.

"Sit." I gesture to the chair. "Show me what you've got done."

I'm not a monster, contrary to popular belief. I am, however, laser focused, and I always get what I want.

Elisa opens her laptop and reviews with me the letter that she's compiled. I make a few suggestions and tweaks, before having her email me the final version, which I will send out to all staff members.

"Is there anything else?" Elisa asks, although it's obvious it's more out of necessity than desire. She wants to run back to her desk and get as far from me as possible.

"Yes, you're going to be my executive assistant in addition to your acquisitions responsibilities."

"Excuse me? Isn't there someone else better qualified for that role?"

She's not wrong. It's not that her experience is limited or lacking. It's more a matter of the two of us working side-by-side being dangerous. Not that we'll wind up in bed together. One of us is more than likely to end up dead.

I force a smile. My eyes crinkle as I fold my arms across my chest.

Her laptop rests on my desk, and I try to seem like I'm not enthralled with having her as my EA, keeping her on her toes, and reporting to me. There's something highly satisfying about getting even with the woman who snuck out on a date.

Was that the first time she'd done something so rude, or is that a regular occurrence? When she isn't enjoying herself, does she usually up and leave?

Do I need to worry that she'll be looking for another job?

"While there is a hiring freeze because I'm not intending to bring in a new Executive Producer, I'm willing to offer you a twenty percent salary increase for working directly under me. You will have additional responsibilities, but I can assure you that the bulk of your work will continue to be with the acquisitions department."

"And if I turn it down?"

"You won't," I say a little too boldly. "Either way, Miss Emerson, you are working for me."

Her pink tongue darts out to the side of her lip, contemplating my offer. "Can I think about it?"

"You have twenty-four hours."

Should I have offered her more money to EA for me? I hate to admit that I don't even know what she makes, and I'm not about to ask her, either. I'll go to HR later and do a little investigative digging to see if my twenty percent offer was good enough.

"Is there anything else?" she asks. It's obvious she doesn't want to be in the same room as me; she can barely look me in the eye.

I consider bringing up our evening, her bailing, but think better of it. Now is not the time to be sore for the way she treated me. There are plenty of single ladies in Manhattan. Besides, dating a coworker and, better yet, an employee, is frowned upon. And the fact that I'm CEO and no longer just an employee. Nope. I will not be pursuing Miss Emerson.

"That depends. Do you plan on being of assistance? Are you going to run to the bathroom and leave me with everything, including the bill?"

Okay, for the record, I didn't intend to say those words. I swore to myself I wouldn't and then it comes out unwillingly because she riles me up inside. Just looking at her stirs emotions I shouldn't have brewing.

Her mouth drops and her eyes widen. "That is highly inappropriate," Elisa says. And she's right.

But I don't care.

I've already crossed the line. I brought it up, and now, it's too late to undo said damage. "I usually wouldn't mind paying for drinks, dinner, a night out with a beautiful woman, but having her escape through the back door on her way to the bathroom is a little juvenile, even for you, Elisa."

"It's Miss Emerson," she corrects me.

Why stop now?

I'm on a rant and I can't help myself.

I step closer, my gaze moving over her body and back up to her face. "The black doesn't suit you, Miss Emerson," I say.

"My dress?" she asks, and glances down at what she's wearing, obviously flustered by my brashness.

"Your hair." I'm no idiot; commenting on a woman's hair, especially if you don't like it, is bad form, but doesn't she deserve a little harshness and scolding? If she's going to work at Blazing Media, she needs to grow a backbone. I don't appreciate women who run out on dates.

She scoffs at my remark, then slams the lid of her laptop shut. "That's it; I quit!" Elisa stands and she's several inches shorter than I am.

If she's trying to be tough or put on a show, it isn't working.

"Fine, I'll find another EA. Someone who can take orders and do as they're told. And one who won't run out the back door when things get tough." I'm not sure whether I'm talking solely about an assistant or a date anymore.

When the hell did the lines get so damn blurred?

Her cheeks are red. It's the only bright color, save for her eyes, that have turned a darker hue of blue. The black dress and haircut would make her easily blend into my office if the lights were off and the blinds closed.

But they're not. The harsh florescent overhead lights make Elisa incredibly pale and washed out with the strong black hue surrounding her. The outside sun pours into the office, shining bright.

"You're incorrigible!" she shouts at me, then grabs her laptop under her arm, and storms for the door.

"Always running, *Miss Emerson*," I say, standing tall over her. "Is that all that you do?"

She spins around and clocks me with a mean right hook.

"Fuck," I mutter, holding my jaw. My eye twitches, and I growl as she rips open the door and storms out of my office.

Maybe I went a little too far.

# THREE

*Elisa*

"WHAT A BOSSHOLE!" I can't help the wave of anger toiling through me as I grab a filing box, toss the contents on the floor and stuff all the crap from my desk inside.

"What happened?" Sloane asks, incredulous, eyes wide, her jaw practically on the floor.

"I can't work for him, Sloane."

"It can't be that bad. What happened?" she asks, glancing in the direction of his office when he stomps out like bigfoot. "Drinks later, on me." Sloane wheels her chair back to her desk, making sure to look busy when Mr. Grump approaches my desk.

Sloane is seated only a few feet away and she can overhear anything in our open bullpen style office. We're neighbors.

The irony isn't lost on me, and I continue to pack the last of my belongings into the box, avoiding the boss's heated glare.

"Elisa, we need to talk."

"I don't have anything to say to you." I'm surprised he hasn't suggested throwing an assault charge at me, and maybe he will. Or at the very least, a restraining order.

I can't even avoid him if I want to, because he lives in my building.

Maybe I should move.

Although that Grumpwad is the new tenant. He should leave, but doubtful that he will. The man probably gets whatever he wants, handed to him on a silver platter. He thinks he's royalty.

What an ass!

I grab the box, toss on my coat, and head for the elevator, ignoring everyone's stares. The email hasn't gone out yet that he's the CEO. Imagine their surprise when everyone discovers that he's not just the new executive producer, he's the fucking boss of this media house.

Let the implosion begin.

I don't glance over my shoulder. I'm not sure what I expect him to do. Chase after me? Yeah, right. This isn't a love story. He's not my prince or knight in shining armor. He's the grumpiest bosshole that I've ever met.

Thankfully, I don't have to work for him another day in my life.

I punch the button on the elevator, wanting the damn ride to come already.

"You should quit assaulting my building," Mr. Grump says. I feel his presence as quickly as I hear him.

He was silent on his approach, but he's brooding and standing over me. Is he trying to make me feel small and insignificant? I already feel like shit. It wasn't bad enough that I hit him but now he's going to harass me all the way to my car?

"It'd be wise for you to back up," I warn.

The elevator doors open but it doesn't feel quick enough. I hurry into the elevator cart, and he leans in, pushing the button for the parking garage. He doesn't step into the elevator.

"Your keycard will be disabled as soon as you leave the parking garage."

"Fine." I shrug like it doesn't matter. "In case you haven't figured it out, I'm quitting, Mr. Grump. I'm not returning to your office, and I swear, if you contact me in my condo—"

"You'll what?" he seethes, glancing me over. Like I'm too small to pose any real danger to him.

"I'll file a restraining order!" I pipe up.

He laughs darkly. "Seriously? You pummeled me, and you're the one wanting an order of protection. Real original, *darling*," he purrs at me.

I punch the elevator door closed button and am relieved when it finally closes. Too bad it's not on his face.

I want to scream. Shout. Beat the hell out of the elevator, but what good will that do?

Weston Grump is a pain in my ass no more. I head to my car, pop the trunk, and drop the box inside. Hurrying around to the front seat, I climb in and hurry out of the parking garage. I don't want another run-in with Grumpwad. Although I'm just as likely to see him in the building where I live.

———

"I couldn't deal with the Grumphole, so I walked out on his first day as CEO," I say. Clare and I met a few months ago when I went to a book conference. She was there because of her love of reading. I was there to spot talent and find the next great book to become a movie. Clare is a nanny and soon-to-be mother to this sweet little girl, Amelia.

"Oh my gosh!" Clare squeals. "And you said you punched him?"

"What?" Sloane's jaw drops. It's the three of us grabbing drinks to celebrate my freedom. I feel bad for Sloane, having to put up with his antics, but at least she didn't try to date him.

I guess Sloane missed that part of the story. I had called Clare to tell her that I punched my new boss, who happens to be my bad date from last weekend, and can she do drinks because I need to vent.

"Yeah, I may have clocked him in the jaw when he brought up the date from hell. And get this, he didn't apologize about my hair catching on fire, or the way he kept checking out the blonde, or staring at his phone. No. He was mad that I left his ass and made him pick up the check. Which was his anyways, since I didn't touch the food and he ordered for the table."

"Table, like there were more than the two of you on the date?" Clare asks, trying to catch up.

"No, it was just us. But he tried to order for me. Who does that?" I ask.

Clare grins. "I think it's rather hot when a guy orders for me."

"On a first date?" I ask. "It's bossy and presumptuous. How does he know that I'm not vegan? He ordered so much cheese. Oh my gosh, I couldn't even eat the food that he ordered."

Sloane takes a long swig from her daiquiri. "Sounds complicated. And by the way, you left Weston in a terrible mood when you quit. All day, he was moping and impossible to placate."

"That's how he is all the time, I'm sure of it. That's why his last name is Grump!"

"It isn't," Clare says, and bursts into laughter. "Oh my gosh, thank god Levi's last name isn't Grump. I couldn't handle that, becoming Mrs. Grump. No way!"

I grin, happy to talk about anything else after my vent. "The big day is approaching. Are you excited?" I grab her hand, admiring the engagement ring that Levi put on her finger. He's the head of the Luxenberg hotel chain and owns Luxenberg Enterprises. He's also wealthy beyond compare.

"A little nervous," Clare confesses, "but I love him, and I'm excited to become Amelia's mother. I mean, I know I'll be her stepmom, but it's still huge. Levi is having me sign legal documents to ensure that if anything happens to him, I'm responsible for her care."

"He must really trust you," Sloane says, sipping her frozen drink.

I elbow Sloane. "Of course he trusts her; they're getting married, and she's Amelia's nanny. I mean, what's not to trust?" To Clare, I add, "You're great with kids. If I had children, I'd trust you with mine."

"When's the wedding?" Sloane asks.

"In a couple of weeks. Which reminds me, do you have your dress?" Clare asks. She's having me stand in as a bridesmaid for her wedding. They're planning something intimate at the cabin they just bought, which seems ironic for a billionaire. But it's what Clare wants, nothing flashy, and I get the impression Levi prefers it that way as well.

"I do, but I can't believe you're going to have an outdoor wedding in winter!" I squeal.

"Are you crazy?" Sloane asks. "Like here, in New York?"

"We're doing a very quick ceremony outside. There will be outdoor heaters, those torches that are propane and portable, to help keep everyone warm during our vows. The reception will be inside, and oh my gosh, I didn't tell you about *my* dress," Clare says.

"No, you didn't." I'm still surprised she has me as part of the wedding party. We've only been friends for a few months, but I couldn't say no.

"It's black."

"You have a black wedding dress?" Sloane's jaw drops.

I laugh and nod. "Clare isn't very traditional."

"Neither is Levi, which is perfect," she says. "He's fine with whatever I want, not that I've let him see the dress. That would be bad luck. Besides, I've done the white gown with a giant wedding, and that didn't work out."

"I didn't realize you were previously married," I say.

Clare waves her hand dismissively. "Long story. He was a narcissistic ass who controlled every inch of my life. From what I wore to whom I could visit. That's when Levi and I met, when I came to New York after my divorce was finalized. I needed a place to stay, there was a mix up and I kind of insinuated that he kidnapped his daughter."

"No way!" Sloane gasps.

"Well, Amelia did say that he wasn't her father. I was tipsy and, well, they'd just been acquainted so she was a bit confused about the situation, and the rest is history!" She finishes her mocktail and orders another.

"Are you pregnant?" I ask. Clare is gorgeous and full of curves. She doesn't appear to be showing, but the fact that she's not drinking alcohol on a girls' night out at the bar has me questioning her reasons.

"No," Clare says with a laugh. "But we're trying. We've been trying for a while. And I'm ovulating, so I don't want to have any alcohol in case we try conceiving tonight."

"You slut," I tease. "Sleeping with a man who's about to be wed!"

"My fiancé." Clare chuckles. "Oh my gosh, don't tell me you're saving yourself for your wedding day because—"

Sloane cuts her off. "Mr. Grump just walked in."

"No way!" Clare's eyes widen, and she turns her attention to the door. "Which one?"

For a girl who's completely sober, she's still really loud. However, the bar is rather crowded and noisy. Someone recently turned up the music, which made everyone have to shout louder if they wanted to talk.

"The hottie in a white dress shirt and black tie. Thick black hair," Sloane points him out without literally pointing at him.

Clare's attention lands right on Weston. "Wowzers, he's hot. I mean, he's not as hot as *my* fiancé, but damn. He could totally be an Italian Stallion in the sheets."

"Or a Grumpwad freak," I interject, and glance away. I don't want him seeing me. "Can we switch seats?" I ask, wanting them to shield me from his view.

"He can't be that bad?" Clare quips.

"No, he is," Sloane says. "He was awful after you left. Demanding an insane workload be completed within the hour. He gave me six new projects to do in addition to the regular workload, which is already insane. Like the guy doesn't understand that research is often involved. Half the office staff quit."

"No way," I gasp, and cover my lips.

"I want to quit, but I can't afford to walk out," Sloane says.

"Yeah, me either." I finish my martini, and while I want another, I don't want to risk wandering up to the bar and coming face-to-face with Mr. Grump. "I need to find another job, pronto."

"You will," Clare says. "I can talk to Levi and see what openings we have available."

"That's sweet. I'm going to apply to some other media houses first. If that doesn't pan out, I might take you up on it," I say. I love working in acquisitions, specifically in romance literature. Hotel marketing doesn't feel as energetic and inspiring, but honestly, I will take whatever is necessary to pay the bills.

But I do have a couple of months' salary saved so I can try to apply, and if that doesn't work out, I can always circle back to Clare for help.

"Just let me know; don't be shy," Clare says.

"This girl shy?" Sloane chuckles and points at me. "Not even close. She got into it with the boss. Are you sure you want her working for your fiancé?"

I smack Sloane's arm. "You're terrible!"

"I'm just kidding, I swear. You deserve to find a job with a boss who adores you, worships you, and pays you what you deserve," Sloane says. "Seriously, I'm glad you quit when you did."

"Why's that?" I ask.

"Because it made everyone realize how awful a boss he is, and I just keep hoping that he resigns or hires someone else to manage the company and he's not so hands-on, like how his father used to run the media house," Sloane says.

"He's too much of a jerk to walk away and let someone else run the company." I run my finger over my empty martini glass.

"Do you want me to grab you another drink?" Clare asks. "You're avoiding the bar because of him, aren't you?"

I hate how easily she can read me. "I am," I say with a laugh, staring down at the table. "I shouldn't care, I should stalk right up to him and tell him to go fuck himself."

"You kind of did that in the office already," Sloane says. "Everyone was watching the two of you at the elevator. It was heated and intense. We were taking bets whether he was going to kiss you."

"What? You're crazy."

"I've never seen chemistry like that before," Sloane says. "It was wild and overwhelming." She fans herself.

"He's a dick, seriously, not worth the trouble. Even if he is gorgeous," I mutter.

"Okay, second round it is," Clare says, and climbs out of our booth to head to the bar and order another round of drinks for the three of us.

"I'll help her carry the drinks back to the table," Sloane says, and climbs out of the booth to help Clare once the order is complete.

I groan, not wanting to be left alone. And for good reason. Mr. Grump glances back at the bar, and his eyes land on mine.

He grabs his glass of beer, or whatever the hell he's drinking, and raises it toward me with a nod. Why the hell is giving me a smile? Like he's happy that I'm here, wallowing in my own self-made misery.

Okay, well, some of it was self-made. I did land a physical blow to Mr. Grump, but he said quite a few inappropriate and unnecessary remarks to me in his office. Still, fighting and being aggressive isn't the answer. My parents would not be proud of me.

Hell, I'm not feeling too proud of myself, either, right now.

Mr. Grump pushes himself off his stool and heads toward me.

Oh, hell no. I'm scowling, and I'd really like that martini, even if it only makes it into Grumpwad's face. It'd be a waste of a perfectly good martini but well worth the twelve dollars for a drink.

"Elisa," he says, giving a nod. Like he's happy to see me. He can't be happy. I'm not happy to see him.

"What do you want, Grumpface?" I mutter, my fingers grazing over the wood table. I glance past him at Sloane and Clare. They are holding the drinks and whispering to each other, probably deciding what to do.

If they could read my mind, tossing it in his face would be my first choice.

But Sloane still works for the jerk, and I doubt she's ready to say goodbye to her job. At least the money, she's not ready to part with yet.

"Real original, Elisa," he says, and his eyes tighten. One hand is tight around his glass of beer, the veins protruding in his arm, like he just might squeeze it a little too tight, and it'll shatter at any moment.

"What do you want?" I assume he wants something, or else he'd be leaving me alone. "Looking to get the last word in? I hear half the staff quit today."

"Half the acquisitions staff," he says with a shrug. "Makes it easier for me. Less people I have to lay-off."

"You're an asshole," I mutter, and raise my arm, gesturing for my friends to come back with the drinks and rescue me.

Sloane is shaking her head no, and Clare is giving me a kissy face.

What the hell? I'm not smooching the douche. *My drink* I mouth to the girls, but they ignore me.

"Looks like you're fresh out of martini. I'd offer to buy you another drink, but you might not stick around until it comes," Mr. Grump says.

"What do you know about sticking around until anything *comes*," I purr. "You're probably a two-minute man."

He snorts under his breath and sips his beer, his eyes raking over me. I swear the man is undressing me with his gaze, and I shift uncomfortably.

"What do you want?" I ask. "Did you come over here to gloat that you got rid of me without even having to pay severance?"

His brow furrows, and he's silent. After a moment, he glances down at the empty glass. "How many of those have you had?"

"Why?" I glare up at him.

"I'm just deciding whether you're a mean drunk or just mean all the damn time." He takes another swig, this time finishing the last of his beer. He slams the empty glass on the table with a purpose.

"All the time when I'm around you."

He places both hands on the table, his head leaning down, invading my personal space. The heat radiates between us, sizzles like electricity, and I feel pulled toward him.

I shouldn't want to kiss him, but his proximity does something to me. Maybe it's the pheromones and his scent that make me lean in and gravitate toward him like a celestial body that I can't escape.

He's a black hole about to suck me in and steal my last breaths of air.

His lips lower as he hovers over me, and I stare up at him, snarling with disgust. But my body isn't responding the way my mind wants it to.

My heart flutters like it did when he first asked me out, and my insides are warm and tingly. I feel betrayed by my own internal reactions that I can't control.

A soft puff of air escapes my lips, and he's just standing there hovering, bathing me in his scent. I want to find it repulsive, like I find him impossible to bear, but instead, I lean toward him. "You're a Grumpwad," I say, staring at him, daring him to fire back his best shot at me.

"You make me that way, *sweetheart*." There's a wicked grin on his face.

"Don't call me *sweetheart*," I seethe, and clench my fists. My top lip snarls at him.

"I'll call you whatever I damn well please," Mr. Grump says with a smirk, and his dark-brown eyes flicker with mirth. The man needs an attitude adjustment.

I will not hit my boss.

I will not hit my ex-boss.

I will not hit anyone.

I repeat the silent mantra, trying to remind myself that violence isn't the answer. Even if I want to pummel this man to the floor and dominate him.

Shit.

Where did those lurid thoughts come from?

I tilt my head past him, looking for my friends. Clare and Sloane have now taken up residence at the bar, drinking my martini.

Gah!

Some friends they are, leaving me with Mr. Grump.

"Your friends aren't coming to save you," he says.

He's too damn astute. "Yeah, well, I didn't like them much anyhow," I mutter under my breath. Not that I'm throwing away two friendships over the shit that they just pulled, but they will get an earbashing later.

Why does he rile me up inside? My tongue darts out and I swipe my top lip. Unlike earlier today, when my mouth felt like a cactus and prickly, I realize that he's staring at my lips. Was he doing that before? Or is it the alcohol that's making him drop his guard and lose the hidden façade of tough guy that he portrays oh so well?

When I realize he's staring at my lips and leans in, I do it again. This time I let my tongue slowly trail over my bottom lip.

Mr. Grump growls at me and lunges forward. His lips nearly touch mine. But he has some restraint buried deep that comes out, stopping him from kissing me.

Damn his self-control.

Wait?

Why do I want him to kiss me?

He's the ultimate grump. The biggest ass on the planet, and I'm getting feelings for him? No.

Absolutely not.

I refuse to let the butterflies be anything more than a result of anger and adrenaline.

Of course, he's hot, especially with that smoldering look in his eyes, but that's all it is. The minute he opens his mouth, it's gone. Caput. He's the devil.

"You're responsible for half the acquisitions team walking out, Miss Emerson."

"We're back to this again?" I say, and pout.

Am I disappointed that he turned the tables back on me and is bringing up what happened at the office? Yes, absolutely. I wanted him to kiss me.

No.

I wanted him to want to kiss me.

That's it.

I want him to desire me.

Fantasize what it would be like with me.

But I'm not letting him touch me.

He doesn't get to worship this body, heart, or soul. I don't belong to him, or anyone else for that matter, and he's never going to get the opportunity to see me naked.

And if he thinks he can kiss me or make me weak at the knees, boy, does he have another thing coming. Like a fist to the face.

I grimace.

*No more violence.*

Okay, I know, I need to chill the hell out. But it's hard with Grumpwad breathing down my neck.

"Cat's got your tongue? I've never known you to be speechless," he whispers, hovering above me.

"Do you have a thing for stealing a woman's personal space?" My hand reaches for his chest and I push back, but in doing so, my fingers graze his tie.

Dammit. The things I could imagine, yanking his tie, pulling him down to me, feeling his body cover mine.

Or even better, using his tie to restrain his arms, watching him shudder as I run my fingers over his bare body.

Grumpwad's eyes flicker, and I pray that he hasn't noticed me getting aroused by his presence. It's just anger and emotion, not sexual desire.

I don't desire him. He's just decent looking.

He's a ten out of ten, but he's undatable. He's arrogant. Domineering. And if that's not bad enough, his name is Mr. Grump!

He clears his throat and backs off, standing up taller and straighter. Like a spell has just been lifted, he shakes his head and walks away.

What the hell?

Clare and Sloane have been watching us the entire time. The minute he jets from the table, they're bringing the rest of their half-consumed cocktails and mocktails to the booth.

I grab mine from Clare, downing the martini in a matter of seconds. My cheeks burn, and the rest of me feels alight.

"Wow, that's Mr. Grump?" Clare says, her mouth hanging open.

"He's insufferable!" I say, and bunch my hands into fists.

"He's kind of hot," Clare whispers, and glances at him. His back is to us as he orders another drink at the bar.

"Any sexiness is quickly replaced by his personality. Trust me," I say.

"She isn't wrong. I had to work with him, and he's no picnic to be around," Sloane says. "But he was looking at you like a feral lion in heat."

"Is that even a thing?" I finish the last of my martini and gesture for Sloane to switch places with me. This time I'll go to the bar and grab myself another drink. It can't be any worse than what I just dealt with from Mr. Grump.

"She's going back for seconds," Clare quips as she watches me saunter toward the bartender.

Mr. Grump is perched on a stool, nursing his drink when I breeze up beside him. I ignore him, so maybe he'll get the hint.

"Martini," I say to the bartender.

"What's that, number three?" Mr. Grump asks.

"Why are you counting?" And while it is the third drink, it could have been more if I'd gotten started a lot earlier. But I didn't. I waited for Sloane and Clare to show up before starting this party.

"You should be careful. Alcohol poisoning is a serious issue," Mr. Grump says.

"Oh my gosh, loosen up, *Old Man*. You're worse than my father."

His eyes wince, and I realize perhaps bringing up a parental figure wasn't the best choice of words, given his stepfather just passed away.

Shit.

I almost feel bad for the guy drinking alone until he opens his mouth and speaks, reminding me why I quit my job.

"Old Man?" he repeats, shifting in his seat and turning to face me. "You keep chasing this Old Man," he says with a smirk.

"In your dreams." I take my martini and hurry back to my friends, needing to get away from Weston Grump as quickly as humanly possible before he consumes me and enraptures me with his wicked charm.

There's something about him, not only in the way he carries himself, but in how he commands a certain authority, that is captivating.

"Wow, didn't get enough of him the first time, you had to go back for seconds," Clare says with a giggle.

It's amazing to me that she's drinking mocktails, but at least one of us is staying sober tonight. She can keep me from doing anything stupid, although it isn't like she was incredibly helpful when Mr. Grump brought himself over to the table.

"Trust me. I've had more than I ever need."

"I'm not so sure," Clare says. "He was practically all over you in the booth. Did you two kiss? He got so close that I couldn't tell."

"Do you think I'd kiss that jerk?" I sip my martini, and both girls are staring at me.

"So, that's a no?" Sloane asks.

"He was the worst date. I'd never kiss him. Ever. Not even if we were the last two people on Earth. The world will perish first."

Clare takes a long drink of her mocktail. "Wow, you've really thought about it. Haven't you?"

"No!" My cheeks burn but not for the reason that they think. He riles me up.

"I think it's kind of endearing, the banter," Clare says.

"You would," Sloane chuckles, "you don't have to work with him."

Clare points at me. "Neither does she anymore."

"Don't remind me," I say. I hang my head in my hands. I need to start looking for a new job first thing tomorrow.

"I'm not sure if you know this, Elisa, but when Levi and I first met, we hated each other. I mean, well, he hated me. I tried to get him arrested." Clare snickers.

Is there any chance that I can get Weston Grump in handcuffs?

Crap.

Why is my mind suddenly imagining doing naughty things to him? I wince and finish the rest of the martini. That ought to help.

While Clare's already told me the story in confidence, she was also trashed and probably doesn't remember much of that night. "He'd kill me if I told anyone. But it's our meet cute."

"Your what?" Sloane asks, scrunching her nose.

"The first time that we met. Anyways, sometimes the best love stories don't start out where two people are madly in love," Clare says.

"Oh, he's mad, all right," I mutter.

"And you're mad for him," Sloane says into her daiquiri glass.

"I heard that!" I elbow Sloane. "You're unbelievable."

"And you've finished your martini. Buy us another round."

I groan. It's not the money. I'd happily pay for all the drinks tonight. Of course, having a job would be beneficial to help with that, but it's waltzing back over to the bar and standing right next to Mr. Grump again.

"Are you girls trying to torture me?" I ask.

"Maybe," Clare says. "It's fun to watch your face turn bright as a tomato."

My eyes widen in horror.

"Don't worry, it's not that bad. He probably thinks it's cute," Sloane interjects.

"You guys are going to kill me. I swear, I should just step out in front of traffic right now."

Clare laughs and finishes the last drop of her mocktail. "Don't be so dramatic. Go get us another round before I have to get home to Levi."

"All right, Miss Bossy Pants," I joke, climbing out of the booth.

"Save your nicknames for your grumpy ex-boss," Clare calls after me.

I groan as I head up to the bar. Why is it the only empty spot is once again next to Weston Grump?

Is the universe trying to torture me?

I realize he's hot. I don't need a reminder, but I could use without talking to him. Just let me have my eye candy, three drinks, and get out before it's too late.

"Missed me?" Mr. Grump says, turning slightly on the barstool.

"Do you always drink alone? Or is it because you chase all the cute girls away?"

His brow tightens, and he gestures the bartender over, ordering himself another beer. I'm kind of relieved he's not ordering another flaming drink like Friday night.

That is one experience I never want to do-over.

"I'll have you know I could get any girl in the bar," he says.

"Any girl?"

"Minus present company and your entourage."

Damn, it would have been fun to watch him flirt with Sloane or Clare and get turned down. There's zero chance either of them would be interested in returning the sentiment.

"How about her?" I say, and nod toward the girl at the end of the bar counter. She's got blonde hair, which I've surmised is his type.

"What about her?"

"You said any girl." Okay, I have to admit I picked the one girl that seems not the least bit interested in men. She's with another woman, and she's wearing a pride shirt, so I'm hoping that she's not attracted to the male species.

"How about I pick my own dates?"

"Then I guess you can't get any girl." I smirk proudly, and the bartender hands me the bill. I slide my credit card over to pick up the tab for the three drinks.

"I've got it," Mr. Grump says, putting his card on the tray.

"What? You're not buying our drinks. I don't need handouts."

"You don't have a job."

Why does he have to remind me that I quit this morning?

Is he going to remind me next that I sucker punched him?

I ignore his remark. "Are you scared of a little bet?"

"What are we talking?" Mr. Grump asks. "A date. A kiss. Her phone number?" He doesn't back down, that's for sure.

I pause, considering the options. "Kiss her." I'm ready to watch him get cold-cocked twice in one day.

"That's it? I just have to kiss her?" The smile on his face is far too smug. He's confident in his abilities to knock a woman off her feet. "And since it's a bet, if you win, I buy your drinks."

That seems easy enough, and I suppose I can let him put the three drinks on his tab. What's the harm?

"And if you win?" I ask. My stomach flutters; I'm afraid of what he'll want in return.

"A second date with you."

"You're sadistic," I say. Is he seriously chasing me for a second date? We hate each other.

"Probably, but my ego got bruised when you bailed. I promise that there won't be any alcohol lit on fire. Well, intentionally, anyways."

I stare at him, dumbfounded by his suggestion. "You're not going to win."

"Then, I see no problem with the bet. And we should make it a little more interesting," Mr. Grump adds.

Inwardly, I'm groaning. "What?" I ask.

"If she gives me a little tongue action, you come back to work for me."

Is he insane? He must be to think that I care. "Why? So you can torment me indefinitely? No thanks."

"I haven't gotten to the good part if you win," he says, letting it hang in the air, and I glance again at the woman seated down the bar. There's no way that she's going to kiss him, especially with tongue.

And while Mr. Grump is gorgeous and drop-dead sexy, the minute he opens his mouth, he'll ruin it. "And what's that?" I take the bait. "You give me your job and let me run the company?"

He offers a wry grin. "I like your sense of humor, but that's not a possibility."

"Too bad, I thought this was going to get interesting. Besides, I knew you couldn't get her to kiss you."

I swear I hear him growl under his breath. "Deal."

Seriously?

My mouth hangs agape, and he shoves his suitcoat at me while he rolls up the white sleeves of his dress shirt to his elbows.

I try not to stare at his arms. The man is all muscle, and I imagine his biceps are thick, but they're hidden beneath the cotton material. He's still wearing his tie, jet black, not a hint of color. It seems fitting. The man is plain and boring. Although even looking basic, he's still got style.

I'm left standing at the bar while he strides across the space like a man on a mission. Except I don't want to watch him kiss some random girl in a bar. My hands bunch into fists as I clench his suitcoat and wrinkle the hell out of it.

He strolls up to her, whispers something into her ear, and she bites on her bottom lip coyly.

She can't be falling for it.

He's handsome but he's arrogant.

Smug.

Impossible to deal with, but she doesn't have to deal with him every day. All he has to do is convince the girl to kiss him.

I should have sized her up a little closer. Is she wearing a wedding or engagement ring? She's too far across the bar to notice her jewelry.

Mr. Grump glances back at me, grins, and winks.

My stomach flops as the girl grabs him by the tie and pulls his lips to hers in a searing lip-lock. There's definitely tongue involved, and I can't watch the rest.

I need air.

The bar is hot and suffocating.

The room spins and my stomach churns.

I do not want to get sick, not in front of Weston, although I doubt the man would notice, since he's smooching with that girl.

I hightail it out of the bar, not caring that I'm ditching Clare and Sloane. They can fend for themselves.

Sweat trickles my brow. The cold night air is a welcome relief from the heat of the bar and the moment I just witnessed between the two of them.

I shouldn't care.

I hate him. He was the absolute worst date I've ever been on and he's the reason I quit my job.

But watching his mouth shoved up against another girl's, his hands in her hair, and hers around his lower back, it was too much.

I bunch up his expensive suitcoat and stalk down the street, offering it to a homeless man. I could have thrown it in the garbage, but someone should get better use out of it.

Anger simmers, and my hands clench, the more that I think about his hands on her face, in her hair, pulling her closer, like he was enjoying it.

I want to throw my head back and scream up at the heavens for bringing me such torment. And he lives in my building. How am I going to face him?

I'm going to have to move. That's the only explanation. Pack up my stuff, box it, and sell the condo. Because I can't face him every day.

Not if he's kissing other girls, and what if he brings one of them back to his place?

What if he brings *her* back to his place tonight?

I despised Mr. Grump when I quit Blazing Media, but now I absolutely hate him. Nothing can change my mind or make me think anything different.

Why was I so naïve to take his bet?

He'd never let me run the company. It was all hogwash, telling me anything to convince me to go along with his plan.

And why?

So that I could watch him kiss another girl?

"Elisa!" Sloane hurries outside, and Clare is right behind her, chasing me down on the sidewalk. "What happened?"

"I'm an idiot," I say, pinching my eyes shut. "I lost a pretty big bet."

"What?" Clare steps forward and pulls me into her arms for a hug. "Whatever it is, it can't be that bad. And he's an asshat for kissing another girl."

They saw that kiss.

I might die from embarrassment, and it wasn't like I kissed Weston Grump. But I hate that I care, that he stoked a fire inside of me and then waltzed off to let it simmer.

I groan, and my heart is crying, but my eyes are dry. "It's horrible. The absolute worst," I say, and I just want to go home and grab a tub of ice cream and wrap myself in a warm blanket.

"Do you want me to go back into the bar and throw a beer in his face?" Sloane asks. "Because I'll totally do that for you."

That wins me a smile, but it fades the minute I catch sight of Weston exiting the bar.

There's a crowd behind him, and I swear if *she's* leaving with him, I'll throw a fit.

I'm being childish and immature. I shouldn't have suggested that he kiss her, but I thought he had zero chance.

I made a horrible assumption, based on her t-shirt, that she had zero interest in boys. That was my mistake.

Sloane and Clare step in front of me protectively.

"You need to turn your butt around and go home," Clare says. She points at Weston's chest and pokes it as he steps into her personal space, trying to get to me.

"She's right," Sloane says. "What kind of a man kisses one girl at a bar while flirting with another?"

His gaze tightens, and he glances past them, staring at me.

I want to look away, but his stern eyes burn right through me. "The kind who insists on a bet. Ladies, if I may, I'll walk Elisa home."

"Are you insane?" Clare asks, her hand pushing him back several feet, putting distance between us. "You just kissed another girl, and you want to walk Elisa home? That's not cool."

Weston's eyes burn at me. "Is that what you told them?"

I open my mouth, but no words come.

Sloane steps up, speaking for me. "She doesn't have to say anything. We saw you kiss that girl in the bar."

"It was a bet. One that your sweet and innocent Elisa suggested."

Clare and Sloane glance back at me for confirmation.

Clare's brow is knitted. "He's not serious?"

Sloane steps closer and gives me a hug. "Please tell me he's a liar," she whispers into my ear. "I'll quit my job with you. We can face job hunting together."

I don't want Sloane to do that because of what I did. "No," I say, "he's not lying. I should talk to him alone."

"Are you sure?" Clare asks, reaching for her purse. "I have pepper spray if you need it."

"I'll be fine. I don't need to assault him for the kiss. I told him to do it."

Clare's eyes widen, and she takes a step back. "Okay, but if you need anything, you call me. Can you get home all right?"

"I'll walk her home," Weston says.

Sloane cringes and glances from Weston to me. She's waiting for me to say something, but what is there to say? I royally screwed up this time. "He lives in the same building. It's fine."

"He's your next-door neighbor?" Sloane's mouth dropped, having missed that epiphany earlier.

"Don't worry, it's not permanent," Weston interrupts, hearing our goodbyes. I hug Sloane and Clare before they head off for a cab together.

I glance at Weston and consider making a break for it, but it's not like he doesn't know where I live.

Never date your next-door neighbor.

# FOUR

*Weston*

WHY DID I take Elisa's suggestion and go with it?

It's not like I'm innocent. Yes, I kissed the girl Elisa bet me that I couldn't kiss. But it wasn't like there was even a hint of attraction from either of us.

I offered her one hundred thousand dollars, and when she said no, I upped it to half a million. That was enough for her to grab me by the tie, and the rest should be history.

I won the bet.

Elisa never set any rules in place about payment, and there was no chance that I was going to turn over a billion-dollar corporation to a girl in acquisitions.

It wasn't a bet that I could lose.

And it was worth the five hundred thousand large ones. Not because I enjoyed the kiss, but I was hoping to catch a glimpse of Elisa's shocked face.

But instead, the moment that I ended the tongue duel, I glanced over my shoulder, and she was gone.

I cut a very large check to a lucky lady at the bar before following Elisa's friends outside in search of her.

Worst case scenario, I could waltz up to her front door and demand she follow through on the bet. While I contemplated keeping it to just a single date, having her work under me is much more inspiring.

I need an executive assistant, someone who can handle my bullshit and be honest with me. If an idea I have is shit, I need someone I trust to tell me that to my face. Not behind my back.

And Elisa is a mystery. Maybe hiring her isn't the best move for the company, but it's what I want. She knows the industry, and she's been around for several years.

I did a little background digging, and she's overqualified for her current position with us in acquisitions. She's been a huge part of the recent success of the business. And the twenty percent raise I offered her for extra work wasn't unreasonable.

She could be playing hardball, but I don't get that impression. Elisa wouldn't have walked out if it was about the money, not without having another job available.

But none of it matters.

I wait for her friends to say goodbye and disperse, leaving Elisa and me alone. We're only a few blocks from the condominium complex.

It's cold outside, and I really wish I had my jacket to help warm me up. I didn't bring anything warmer than a suitcoat, and that seems to have been abandoned.

"Where's my coat?" I ask, unrolling my sleeves, making them long again. It's not enough, but it keeps the direct chill off my skin.

"I gave it to someone who needs it," Elisa says with a smirk. "It's cold tonight."

"Tell me about it," I mutter under my breath.

"Why? You should be plenty warm after having that girl's hands all over you."

I stop walking and grab Elisa by the arm, turning her to face me. "Jealous?"

She inhales a shaky breath. "No." Turning, she shrugs out of my grasp. I don't force my hold, letting her take a step back.

But I'm right next to her. She's not walking home at this hour alone. Even if we're in a nice part of town, I'm not risking anything happening to her.

"In case you forgot, you were the one who suggested I kiss her with tongue and picked out the girl."

"Well, you didn't have to enjoy it," she mutters.

"You are jealous." It's the only thing that makes sense. But why does she care?

We had a lousy date together. She quit her job the minute she found out I'm her boss. Granted, I wasn't exactly warm or welcoming, but she didn't have to bail.

"No, I'm not. I just hate losing a bet."

Is that why she ran outside of the bar and wanted to get away from me? Is working for me that torturous a job?

I've never had to manage other employees, let alone an entire company. At least not directly. I had the luxury of hiding behind my computer screen, working as my father.

And now I have to prove myself all over again. Before, I had to prove that my father was capable of doing the work, even though he wasn't, but I had to act on his behalf and make executive decisions in the best interest of the company.

We're not a publicly traded company. There isn't a board of directors or shareholders to whom I'm forced to reveal my hand.

"Well, that's too bad, Miss Emerson," I say, "because you will be coming back to the office tomorrow morning."

She purses her lips and exhales a lengthy sigh. "I suppose I can't talk you out of it. Remind you that we hate one another."

"Hate is a strong word."

What did I do to deserve such distrust? It wasn't my fault the date was a natural disaster. Maybe we're not meant to be anything more than acquaintances, and that's fine with me. Now that I know she works for me, anything else would have to be off-limits.

"Yeah, but it's deserved in this instance," Elisa says.

I step closer, invading every inch of space without physically touching her. "I don't believe you hate me, Miss Emerson. Because if you did, you'd never have run out of the bar after watching that lip exchange."

Her eyes flicker, and the anger that seems to seep into her features disappears just as fast. She's capable of hiding her emotions more than I gave her credit for previously. "Like you said, I just make it a habit of bailing. Which is why I shouldn't come back to work for you."

"Why? Because you'll quit." That doesn't surprise me.

No, what surprised me was Elisa's bold assumption that I'd want to kiss another girl in the bar and that she didn't suggest that I kiss her. That is the only bet that would have left me in a frenzy, and I might have wagered the company and lost it to her.

But there are other nights for more fun and games with Miss Emerson.

My gaze rakes over her body. She's shivering, her grip clutching her purse.

Is it the cold or my proximity that makes her tremble?

I want to be the reason.

But she hates me. Elisa has made it perfectly clear that she wants nothing to do with me. And a woman like that doesn't bend easily to the will of someone strong and powerful.

She's too stubborn to think of her future. The opportunities that she's giving up by leaving Blazing Media.

"I didn't expect you to rescind on a bet." I want to mince words with her, but she's tapping her feet to keep the blood flowing in this chill, and I'm doing my best not to freeze.

Did I mention that I despise winter?

But my father is the reason that I'm still in New York and not living it up on the beaches in Hawaii or the Caribbean. Even the South Pacific would be amazing right now. Anywhere but a New York winter.

It's not as though I can't afford it. I've inherited the company and my father's fortune, moving me from millionaire to billionaire status. It's not all liquidated funds, but I have more than I'll ever need in my lifetime.

And very few people know that about me. I keep my private life quiet. And I don't flaunt my money.

Well, not typically. At the bar earlier was an exception.

I could not lose the bet with Elisa, and I was willing to do anything to ensure I didn't lose. Even if I had to stack the deck, which is pretty much what I did, she can't find out.

Her eyes flinch, and she shivers. "Can we walk? My legs are numb."

I'd pick her up and carry her, but I don't think she'd like that very much. And I don't want another blow to my face. I'm lucky she didn't throw back a hard enough blow to leave a bruise.

"Yes, let's walk and discuss," I say, keeping her pace as we stroll together along the sidewalk.

"I'm not rescinding on the bet. I just don't think you'll be happy with me working under you," Elisa says.

*Working under you.*

Those words play on repeat in my head.

*I'd like to get her under me. Pin her down, show her what it's like to be respected.*

I miss whatever she's jabbering on about for the next couple of streets. We still have a few minutes to go before we're back at the building.

"Did you hear a word I just said?" Elisa asks, glancing at me.

"It's cold. I'm just trying to focus on getting to the condo before I get frostbite."

We approach the last block, but we can't cross the street until the traffic clears or the light turns.

I rub my hands together and blow what I would hope to be warm air into them. It doesn't help.

Why the hell didn't I suggest a cab?

While I usually tolerate the cold, I'm not dressed for this weather. I didn't plan on walking home from the bar, that's why I didn't take my winter coat with me.

She grabs the scarf that's wrapped around her neck and offers it to me, swinging it around and pulling it down around both sides of my neck.

Her gaze lingers for a moment longer than necessary. "Does this make us even?" Elisa asks.

"Giving me your scarf when we're two minutes from home?" It is warm, and it smells uniquely of her scent. It's overpowering and wonderful, a blend of roses and vanilla with a spicy aroma that tickles my nostrils.

I could get used to this smell. I try not to let her notice me breathing her sweet fragrance in as I bring the scarf up around my chin, lips, and nose. It's thick and warm.

"Consider it a peace offering," Elisa says, "since I gave your jacket to a homeless man."

"That was kind of you, even if it was at my expense." The traffic light changes, and we hurry across the street, not because we're worried about getting run over, but we're anxious to get inside a warm building.

The minute we approach the foyer, I grab my wallet, with the keycard positioned on the outside, and press it against the black entry panel to unlock the door. I hold the door open for Elisa, letting her step inside first.

She shivers, and we're both assaulted with a warm gust of heat.

"That's better," she says, digging her keys out of her purse. The heat is turned up quite a bit, but it does feel really good.

We head to the elevator together, and she presses the button for the fourth floor. "You are coming in tomorrow to work," I say. It's not a question.

"Excuse me?" Elisa glances at me. She unzips her jacket and I slowly remove the scarf that she draped around my neck and return the sentiment.

I step into her personal space, wrapping the scarf around her neck, my hands tugging at the ends, keeping her close to me. The gesture is intimate and heated as we stare into each other's gaze.

"You lost the bet, Elisa. You work for me."

Her mouth drops as she stares up at me. "You can't be serious. As you said, I'll just quit."

"Ninety days," I quip. I should have said a year, something more permanent, but I'm not sure either of us can survive that long together.

"I don't know why you even want me, Weston."

It's the first time I've heard her call me by my first name since our date. Ever since that epic disaster, I've been *Mr. Grump,* which gets old and isn't the least bit charming.

Not that I'm attempting to be charming with Elisa. And if she is working for me, there is zero chance that we'll sleep together, ever.

I avoid relationships like the plague. I have a son who needs my focus, not a woman vying for attention. And aren't they all the same?

And marriage is absolutely out of the question. Never in my life, am I committing myself to one woman. It's not because I like a little variety, although it's true I do. I can't trust that whoever that woman is, isn't a gold digger.

Sure, there are prenups that can be signed, but that only covers prior to the marriage. I don't need a woman sneaking in through the side door to get a piece of the empire that my father created.

And while that wouldn't directly be hers, any money earned while married, she would be entitled to a portion of. No thanks.

I prefer my bachelor nights and hookups with random girls who don't know that I have a kid, because I never invite them over.

And there's no chance of them spending the night and not leaving if they don't know where I live.

"Ninety days, and I'll pay you a bonus if you convince the rest of the staff not to quit."

The elevator dings, and Elisa steps out first, heading toward her door. She glances at me over her shoulder. "Is it really that bad?"

Her eyes soften, and her shoulders are less tense. Is it that she's warmed up from the cold or is no longer hostile toward me? Could I be so lucky that her anger isn't directed at me for a change?

"It wasn't pretty when they all walked out."

She laughs under her breath. "Well, Mr. Grump, if you treated any of them the way you treated me at your office this morning, then I don't blame them."

I step closer, forgoing the door to my place. I'll be home soon enough. I have the nanny with Tyler, and at this hour, he's already down for bed.

"It's funny how you blame me when you were the one talking about my cock."

She inhales sharply, and her cheeks blush. "Can we pretend that didn't happen?" She reaches to twirl the strands of her hair.

I won't comment on the gesture. She's nervous, and her gaze flickers down to my lips. "If you can be professional at the office, I certainly can as well."

She exhales a shaky breath and fumbles with her keys. "Very well, I'll see you tomorrow at the office."

"We'll drive together." There's no reason for her not to carpool, and besides, I have a private driver arranged for work.

I refuse to drive in New York City. And while I love driving off-road in the mountains and can tolerate an empty highway, I won't let my blood pressure spike over a traffic jam. I leave that for my driver.

"Are you sure that's appropriate?" Elisa fiddles with her keys. She's ready to go into her condo, and I'll let her, as soon as we knock out the last details for tomorrow. "Besides, will our hours line up?"

"I don't work late nights at the office. If I have work that needs to be done after hours, I do it from home." She doesn't need to know about Tyler. He's the reason that I vow to be home every night for dinner. At least as many nights as possible.

"Okay, I guess we can carpool," Elisa says.

I don't correct her that I have a private driver and am chauffeured around the city. She'll meet Camden tomorrow.

"Goodnight," I say, making sure that she gets into her apartment before I unlock my front door and head inside to check on my little man and kiss him goodnight.

The nanny is already fast asleep in her bedroom. Martha is an older woman in her early sixties. I don't know how she keeps up with Tyler and all his energy, but she helps around the house a lot with chores, laundry, and meal prep.

———

The next morning, I'm awake early and text Elisa that we're leaving in twenty minutes and to meet me downstairs by the front entrance.

Her response is a thumbs-up emoji, and I'll take that as a win, considering who it's coming from. I put on a fresh suit and tie. I'll have to replace the suit coat that I lost, thanks to Miss Emerson giving it away.

Not that I don't help the homeless, I donate clothes to charitable organizations and give a generous monetary contribution as well. But I don't hand over a tailored suit coat that I still wear on a regular basis.

I'm doing my best not to grumble before I've even left the condominium.

I head down to the elevator, and Elisa steps out from her place, just in time for us to ride the elevator together.

It shouldn't be a big deal, we're driving all the way to the office together, but at least in the car, we'll have company. Camden will be there to make sure that Elisa behaves herself. Although, I'm not sure what I'm expecting to happen.

I don't bother with my coat. I'll be staying inside until Camden pulls up, and the car will be warm.

"Good morning," she says, forcing a smile. She's dolled up in a winter hat, gloves, scarf, and purple wool coat. Her cheeks redden when she meets my intense stare.

"Morning," I say, not sure if it's good yet or not. The morning is still young.

"Are you sure it's all right for me to ride with you?"

I push the button for the lobby and wait for the elevator doors to close and for us to descend. "The elevator cart or the car?" I ask, glancing at her.

"Both?" her voice squeaks, and the fact that she might actually be nervous is cute.

"It's fine. We'll just chalk up the past week to Mercury retrograde."

"You believe in that?" Elisa asks. Her eyes widen, and she quirks a sly grin.

I clear my throat. My sister believed in it, up until the very end. "That was my sister's specialty. Not mine." It's the only answer that I provide.

Her brow pinches, and the elevator door slides open. Elisa steps out first, and I follow behind her until we reach the lobby, where I open the door for her and head into the bristling chill.

The car is waiting in the loading and unloading zone, flashers on, and the motor running.

Camden hurries out of the vehicle and comes around to open the back passenger door.

"Ladies first," I say, letting Elisa climb into the backseat. I slide in beside her, and Camden gives me a curious look, but knows better than to ask, especially in front of a woman.

The backseat is plenty warm and helps dispel the icy air outside the vehicle. I shiver, my body warming up from being outside for a few seconds without proper winter attire.

Elisa continues to wear her hat, gloves, and scarf, not including the buttoned jacket. At some point, she's going to sweat to death or start stripping down. I'm taking bets on the disrobing part, although I'd like it to be more than just her winter garments.

Camden climbs into the driver's seat and glances back at me, waiting for me to indicate where I'm dropping off the girl.

I never give anyone a ride except for Tyler and the nanny. Camden is familiar with my close contacts. He never meets my hookups, and quite frankly, there would be no reason for him to, since I don't bring any of the ladies home.

"To the office," I instruct, since Camden hasn't pulled out into the traffic yet.

"Of course, sir," Camden says, and turns off his hazard lights before flipping on his blinker and pulling out into the traffic.

The heat in the backseat is nice and toasty.

Elisa shifts slightly, and I can imagine that she's getting warm. "You mentioned a sister. Do you have any other siblings?" she asks.

Her question catches me off guard. It shouldn't. I brought up Wren. That was my own fault. She died three years ago, and it still cuts deep, like it was yesterday.

"No." A single-word response. It's all I can give her. This woman and I, we aren't friends. I can't give her a part of myself, open up to her, to let her tear me down and destroy me.

"Oh, okay. Will she also have an active role at the media house?" Elisa asks.

"No."

It's all that she gets and all I'm willing to give.

Her mouth closes, and I pray it's the last question she has about Wren.

# FIVE

*Elisa*

THE LONGER I work with Weston, I begin to realize how private a person the man is and how little he reveals of himself.

It was weeks ago when he mentioned having a sister.

Is she alive?

Is she in hiding?

Maybe she has a family of her own and lives in another country. It's strange to me how a father could have two children and give one of them ownership of the company but not both.

Unless she's deceased.

That would explain Weston's lack of an answer or discussion on the matter. Maybe it hurts too much to talk about.

I recognize that it's none of my business, and I should leave it well enough alone, just like him. We ride to and from work together. I handle the acquisitions responsibilities, and in addition, I also am Weston's executive assistant. Which, if I'm honest, sucks.

It's just not a job that I love, and having a grumpy boss doesn't help matters.

But I keep my head down, get my work done, and make sure not to gossip about Weston. And I don't need to gossip about him. There are enough rumors circling about the number of staff who quit and why only one of them returned.

Me.

But HR hasn't called me into their office, and I haven't done anything wrong. I mean, other than that small comment about Weston's dick. It wasn't classy. But I was pissed about how the date went.

Maybe I shouldn't care.

I definitely need to move on.

Swearing off dating because Weston was a terrible date isn't fair to me. One day, I'd like kids, and it's a lot easier to do that with a partner. Especially the raising them part of having kids.

Besides, I like being in a relationship. Having someone to cuddle with every night, curling up against, falling asleep in their arms.

One bad date is just that.

A one-off type of situation. It doesn't have to be the end of the world. Even though it does make me dread dating again. And I don't trust my friends to set me up with anyone on a blind date.

Although Clare did call me recently and tell me that she's putting me at the singles' table at the wedding, hoping I hit it off with one of her fiancé's single friends.

But if he's still single, what's the catch?

Weston is busy in his office, keeping to himself, which is fine with me. It means less handling of his problems and getting more of my work done for the team.

I have a few minutes to myself, so I grab my phone and head for the breakroom. Leaning against one of the walls, I open the dating app on my phone and flip through the countless guys who show up on my screen.

The problem is that even if they're hot and I'm attracted to them, they could be like Weston—a grump and a horrible date. Not to mention my boss.

It's highly unlikely that the boss part will be an issue again. Weston doesn't plan on kicking the bucket and turning the reins over to someone else. Right?

Still, I'm hesitant to date a complete stranger based solely on looks, even if it's just for drinks.

"What are you doing?" Weston's voice startles me as he comes up from behind, and I turn my phone over so that he can't see it.

"N-nothing," I stammer.

He grabs a ceramic mug and pours from a fresh pot of coffee that one of the receptionists made a few minutes ago. The breakroom still smells of fresh coffee beans.

"Does that nothing involve online dating?"

"Not that it's any of your business," I say, and fold my arms across my chest. "But yes, I was looking at hot dates."

"For yourself, or are you one of those friends who sets everyone else up?"

Does he really have to ask?

In his defense, he did ask me out for drinks. I wasn't the one pursuing him, although I had been overly friendly, offering to show him around town if he was new.

Turns out, he wasn't new, just new to the building.

"Don't worry about it." I shy away from answering his question. I don't want him to interrogate me about my type, or worse, to give me hell again for ditching him that first night we went out for drinks.

"So, it's for you," Weston says. He adds a dash of creamer to his coffee and stirs it before taking a sip.

"I didn't say that."

"You didn't have to," he says, his eyes never leaving mine.

I glance away, his stare too intense and bold for me to manage this afternoon. "I should get back to my desk."

"Work can wait. Sit." He nods toward the breakroom table.

This can't be a good idea.

"I have stuff to do," I say, and point back to my desk. "The acquisitions team is counting on me."

"I'm counting on you." Weston's gaze tightens, and he pulls back the chair. It slides across the floor, squeaking in a high-pitched manner, making me grimace.

Did he do that on purpose?

The man loves to torture me.

"Sit." His single word is a command, and I obey.

I pull out the chair and sit on the wooden surface. I wait for whatever it is that he intends to say. Although personally, I don't think now is the best time if we're discussing something intimate like dating.

"I have friends," Weston says.

"You do?" I laugh at the frown forming on his face. "Stop right there if you think you can set me up with one of your friends. That's not going to happen."

Is he crazy?

I don't need a repeat disaster with Weston version 2.0. That would be dreadful.

Weston sips his coffee, his eyes staring straight into my soul. "If I remember correctly, you still owe me a date."

Thankfully, I'm not the one drinking coffee, or I'd have spit it all over him. Unintentionally. "Excuse me?"

"The bet, or don't you remember?" He tilts his head, and there's a set of footsteps approaching the breakroom.

Weston stands, although this time he's quiet with the chair, placing it back as it was, when Sloane steps inside. "Oh, you," he says.

I can't tell if he's relieved or irritated that, whatever he says, she'll side with me.

"Oh, you, too," Sloane says right back to him. "Is this knucklehead bothering you?" She jabs her thumb in his direction.

"No, it's fine. I was just going to head back to my desk. I need to finish the monthly report you asked for," I say to Sloane.

"It can wait," Weston interrupts. "I need to see you, Miss Emerson, in my office."

I follow Weston to his office, and Sloane gives me an apologetic look. I merely shrug, unsure why he wants to bring me behind closed doors unless he plans on reaming me. What'd I do this time?

"Have a seat," he says, and gestures to the empty chair across from his desk. He closes the office door and sips his coffee before sitting behind his desk.

"You should be careful meeting strange men on the internet."

"I don't need you to protect me," I say. I fold my arms across my chest. "I've been taking care of myself forever."

"Even so, there are a lot of men on those apps who aren't good guys," he says, staring at me. Like I'm supposed to know what that means.

"I get it. They just want to hook up. It's cool. Sometimes that's all I'm looking for too."

His jaw drops, and I leave him speechless.

Good.

It's not true, not even in the slightest, but he doesn't have to know that about me.

I want him to think about what he missed out on when he was too busy checking out the blonde and staring at his phone all night. Not to mention the fire incident. Just thinking about it makes me want to swear off dating forever.

"Maybe you don't care who you let into the building, but I do."

"You're worried who I sleep with?" I run my fingers through my hair and drop my head into my hands. "Weston, this isn't an appropriate conversation to have with one of your employees." Has he lost his mind?

"I don't want strange men wandering the halls."

"What the hell? I don't even know how to respond to that," I say, and stand. "I'm not talking to you about my dating life or my sex life, Wes."

"Don't call me that," he growls, and a shiver courses through my body.

I hold up my hand. "I can't deal with whatever this is," I say, and head for the door, trying to hightail it out of his office.

"There you go again, running."

With my hand on the doorknob, I inhale a deep breath. I either face him or do exactly as he's saying, running.

I spin around, and he's closing the distance between us, coming closer to the door.

"I shouldn't have come back here to work under you," I say, and grimace at the double innuendo. Not that I slept with him. I can count the number of guys I've slept with on one hand, and it's not a lot.

I'm not the kind of girl who wants no-strings-attached fun. That's not my style. I prefer romance and passion. I want to be swept up, not swept away.

"What? Why?" Weston doesn't seem to grasp any inkling of why I'm upset right now. "We're a good team. We work well together, and yes, I'm not the easiest person to get along with, but you do a good job."

"That's the first time you've given me any praise."

He tilts his head, his eyes boring into mine. "You have a praise kink?"

My cheeks burn, and I glance away. "That isn't appropriate, Weston. You can't say something like that to an employee."

The corner of his lip turns upward. "I was just kidding."

I don't think he was joking, and even so, that's an HR nightmare. "Your flirting sucks," I say, and stand straighter and taller, like I don't care. It doesn't mean anything. It can roll right off my shoulders, his words.

"Yeah, it probably is a bit rusty," he says, and takes a step back, allowing me the chance to talk with him or dart out of his office.

I contemplate both options but remain by the door.

"You're exhausting, do you know that?" I ask.

"So I've been told." Weston shrugs like he doesn't care what I think, except maybe deep down, it matters to him. He clears his throat and glances at his desk. "Seriously, you've been doing good work around here. I should be complimenting you, especially if that keeps you working under me."

I shift uncomfortably the way he says, *working under me,* like he's in charge of me. And while he is at the office, it still is a bit unsettling to hear from his lips.

Maybe it's because the angrier I get with him, the more I think about him. Dream about him. And those dreams are the type I should not be having about my boss. They keep me up at night when I wake up hot and bothered, imagining his hands and lips on my naked body.

It's why I need to get out, meet some guys, and find a man who isn't my boss or a Grumpwad to date. I stand behind the fact that Weston is a grump.

There's a hint of a smile on his face, like he knows what I'm thinking. But he can't know. It's not possible.

"You still owe me that date," he says.

"And here we go, round and round. Not happening. I came back, and I work for you. I followed through on that bet."

"You followed through on part of it," Weston says. "And I'm serious about bringing strange men home. That's not a very safe thing for you to do."

"Duly noted."

"Just be careful out there." Weston steps forward, and there he goes again, stealing my personal space.

I half expect him to touch me, but he keeps his arms folded tight across his chest. "Be sure to talk with someone for a while online before you meet up with them. And do it in a public place."

"No, I'm going to invite the first guy I match with online straight into my bed." I turn my phone around and unlock it. I open the app, pretending to do exactly as I said, when he snatches my phone from my fingers.

"Give it back." I can't believe him! "Are you twelve?" I ask, and reach for my device, but he's scrolling through the pictures, marking every male as a *no*. "You're deplorable. Just because you can't get laid doesn't mean I shouldn't."

He laughs under his breath. "I see I've rattled you."

"What does that even mean? I'm not a snake."

"I never said you were." Weston glances at my app a little longer than necessary and clicks at the screen before returning my phone to me.

"Did you read all my messages?" I ask in a huff.

"No, I deleted them."

I can't tell if he's serious. He's not smiling, but he looks smug. Like he got exactly what he wanted. I'm just not sure what that was. A rise out of me? Or did he delete any messages that I haven't seen yet? "You had better be joking."

"You shouldn't be on dating apps during company time," Weston says.

"I was on a break and not using the company's resources."

His tongue darts out, and he strokes his jaw. "Keep your private life out of the office, Miss Emerson, and we won't have a problem."

"The only problem I see is you," I mutter, and yank open his office door.

"Excuse me?"

"You heard me, *Grumpwad*."

"That's not even a word."

His gaze is on me as I stalk back to my desk. I let my hips sway and give him a show. Is that what he wants? A little tease? Does he think because we went out once, on the worst date of my life, that I owe him a redo?

Fat chance in hell.

I'll never go out with Weston Grump again. I'd sooner walk over hot coals and then a bed of nails than spend another minute outside of work with him.

As it nears five o'clock, I head to Sloane's desk. "Drinks?" I ask.

"I can't tonight. Don't you have that dress fitting for Clare's wedding?"

My eyes widen. I totally forgot about that. "Shit," I mutter, and glance at my watch. There is no way I'm going to make it across town before the shop closes.

I dial Clare and pray that she will pick up her cell phone.

"You're not here," Clare says. Not even a hello.

"I'm sorry. Mr. Grump got me all riled up, and I lost track of the time." I forego mentioning that I completely forgot I was even supposed to leave early and catch the subway to get across town.

"Shit. I was wondering what happened when you didn't show up twenty minutes ago. My alterations are done, so I'm here, and I can pick up the dress for you. But you need to make sure your dress fits before the wedding. If you don't come in today, the deadline for the alterations is after the wedding. The tailor for the bridal shop won't be able to do it."

"I know. I will find someone to handle it last minute if the dress needs any adjustments."

"Okay, how about I swing by your place with the dress when I'm done? We can have take-out or something, because Levi is out of town on business tonight, and I hate being lonely. I don't know how you do it."

"Thanks," I mutter with a laugh. I know she doesn't mean anything offensive, but it came out a bit harsh.

"My treat for dinner, since you're picking up the gown. What time will you be over?" I ask.

"Not before seven with traffic."

I take the subway home, avoiding Weston. Maybe I shouldn't let what he did bother me, but the man has the uncanny ability to get under my skin. Does he do that with everyone?

Besides, let him think I have a hot date.

I get home quite a bit later than I would with Weston's driver chauffeuring us. Not that traffic is better than the subway, but the trains are running late.

On the way home, I stop for Chinese food take-out and pick up an order for the two of us to share, with quite a bit of leftovers. I make it home before Clare shows up and grab utensils and plates, setting the table.

There's a soft rap at the door, and I pull it back, surprised to find a little boy wandering the hallway.

"Where's your mom?" I ask, bending down to his level.

I glance around, and the door to 4B is wide open.

Isn't that where Weston lives?

"Wes?" I call, and grimace, realizing he lashed out earlier at the nickname I'd given him. "Weston?" I try again.

The little boy points at the open door, and I step inside, glancing around. The condo is clean and tidy. There are dishes on the counter and food on the table for dinner.

"Is your dad home?" I ask.

The little boy, who can't be older than three, shakes his head.

On the floor is a gray-haired woman.

Is that his grandmother?

I rush to her side and press my fingers to her pulse point, looking for any sign of activity while I dig my phone out of my pants pocket, dialing 9-1-1.

I relay that there's an unresponsive woman with no pulse in apartment 4B. I give the address as I begin chest compressions, trying to help.

The EMTs arrive and continue trying to resuscitate the woman while Clare comes up the elevator.

"Are you okay?"

"I'm fine. My neighbor. I think she just had a heart attack. I need to call Weston."

"Why?"

"This is his apartment. That might be his mother." I shuffle the little boy into my place but leave my hall door wide open in case Weston comes home.

I dial his phone, but he doesn't answer.

Of course not. He's probably still mad at me for wanting to have a life outside of work. I text him, hoping that he'll answer me quicker that way.

*Elisa: You have a kid? He's fine by the way, but your mother was taken to the hospital. I found her unconscious in your place.*

*Weston: What the hell were you doing in my home?*

That's his response? Not a simple thank you, or I'll be back soon. I show Clare the text.

"Ouch. He's probably just worried about his mother. But I mean, you did start the text with an accusation." Clare tells it like it is, whether I want the truth or not.

It's too late. I can't unsend the text. He's already read and replied.

Clare, the little boy, and I eat dinner at my place. After the EMTs leave and I got ahold of Weston, I locked my front door.

Mr. Grump knows where I live. Besides, he might be heading straight to the hospital. Although he told me he was on his way home.

"Do you have a name?" Clare asks. She smiles at the little boy as he shakes his head no. "I'll bet you do."

His cheeks redden, and he runs and hides behind the sofa.

I sit on the floor, my back against the opposite wall of the sofa so that I can see the little boy and make sure he doesn't get into anything. "I'm Elisa," I say.

The little boy has the brightest yet darkest eyes I've ever seen. It's such a contradiction, yet he steals my gaze. He's undoubtedly Weston's son. The hair, the smile. Even the same dimple on his right cheek.

He steps backward, smacking into the wall, but he doesn't so much as flinch. He stares at me, and it reminds me so much of Weston that it's uncanny.

Where is the little boy's mother? Weston never mentioned that he was married, but he also neglected to tell me that he had a kid.

I exhale a heavy breath as Clare cleans up our dinner dishes while I keep a watchful gaze on the little one. I'm not chancing he'll get into something and his father will blame me.

I play with my phone, glancing up at the toddler every so often. He watches with curiosity before tumbling at me, trying to wrestle me for the phone.

"Oh, you are just like your father," I laugh as the little boy tries to grab my cell phone.

Clare glances at me over her shoulder. "I think I missed something."

"Wes decided to snatch my phone and delete my dating app messages at work."

"Wait, what? And Wes?" Clare grins. "Wow, you've given him a nickname."

"Only because I know that he absolutely hates it. Yes, I'm that much of a bitch."

"Bitch," the little boy repeats, and grabs my phone from my fingers.

"No, no, no. You can't say that."

There's a firm knock on the front door, and Clare grabs it before I can stand. "Tyler?" Weston says, foregoing any pleasantries.

"He's right over there," Clare says, and points at the two of us on the floor. The little boy is still wrestling for my phone, but the minute he sees Wes, he releases his grip.

"Daddy," Tyler squeals, and runs toward his father.

Weston bends down and sweeps Tyler into his arms, giving him a giant hug and several kisses. It feels like such an intimate moment that I'm invading.

"I'm sorry about your mother. Are you going to the hospital now to see her?" I ask, standing and approaching the two of them.

Clare takes a step back, hanging out in the kitchen, although she can see and hear everything that's going on. My condo isn't huge, but there's enough room for it to be comfortable. Besides, it's just me living here.

"She's not—Martha is Tyler's nanny."

"Oh. I thought nannies were young twenty-somethings out of college."

"That's a stereotype," Clare quips. "I used to be Amelia's nanny."

"Yeah, but you're super young," I say, glancing over my shoulder at Clare.

"Twenty-nine."

I've got five years on Clare. My biological clock is ticking. I return my attention back to Weston. "Is there anything that I can do?" I ask. I'm not sure how to help, but his eyes are dark and worn, his face sullen.

He must be close with Martha.

"I'm going to stop by the hospital and see what I can find out," Weston says.

"Do you want me to watch Tyler?" I ask, having learned his name.

He glances from Tyler to me like he's not sure that's a wise decision.

"I'll stay and help," Clare offers. "I've been watching Amelia since she was five."

Weston's brow tightens. He doesn't look convinced that the two of us can handle one little boy. "Tyler is three, and your place isn't babyproofed."

"Are you asking us to watch him at your place?" I'm not sure what he's getting at. Is he trying to use it as an excuse or mulling the idea over?

"If you're going to be a while," Clare chimes in, "it might be good to stay where he's familiar. Especially if it's his bedtime soon."

"No bedtime." Tyler squirms in Weston's grasp, trying to wiggle free.

Weston emits a heavy sigh. "Are you sure? I can just take him with me."

"No, you can't." I step forward toward the two boys with the cutest dimples I've ever seen. One I could easily fall in love with. The other, that's a thought I shouldn't even ponder. "Hospitals don't let children in to visit, and it'll be his bedtime before you get back. Right?"

"No bedtime," Tyler repeats again.

"Dammit, Elisa."

"Dammit. Dammit. Dammit," Tyler chants.

Weston groans, not pleased but not stopping it, either. I imagine that he's overwhelmed with all that's happening.

"It's fine. We can handle a little boy for a couple of hours," I say.

"I swear I'll be back as soon as I can get an update at the hospital. I'll text you when I hear anything."

Weston escorts Clare into the hallway and to his door while I lock up my place. I shove my phone into my pocket and follow inside. There's a broken dish on the floor that needs to be cleaned up.

Weston hands me Tyler. "I need to clean up this mess before I leave."

"We've got it," I say. "I promise we can handle him while you visit the nanny in the hospital. You should probably get ahold of her family too. Let them know what's going on. I'm sure they'll be worried and want answers as well."

"She doesn't have anyone," Weston says. "And I'm not leaving this mess for you to clean while looking after my son."

His son.

Just hearing the words sets it in stone. I have so many questions, but it doesn't feel right asking, at least not right now. But it's clear that maybe the Grumpwad isn't such a bad guy after all.

The kid certainly takes to him, and maybe there's a softer side to Weston that I haven't seen before today.

Clare cleans up the food that's out on the counter and works on the dishes while Weston picks up the tiny shards of the plate that shattered. He makes sure the floor is safe and spotless, vacuuming the hardwood floor before giving Tyler a bear hug.

Weston gives me a boatload of instructions on his way out the door, instructing me about his bedtime, showing me where his bedroom is, in case I couldn't have figured out that the bright red race-car bed was for a three-year-old.

"Don't go thinking I'm a free babysitter while you get to go on hot dates," I joke with Weston as he's on his way out the front door.

"Not funny, Elisa."

But I swear I catch a hint of a smile playing on his lips.

He's out the door, and it's just the three of us.

Tyler doesn't seem to be overwhelmed when his father leaves, which is a relief. He's busy playing with his own toy phone, which happens to be a real phone that is considerably old. I'm not sure how safe that is for a kid his age, but his father gave it to him.

It's not my place to say anything. Just make sure that he doesn't get hurt.

After Tyler is changed into his pajamas and tucked into bed with a story, I shut off the lights and close his bedroom door, heading to the living room with Clare.

"How long do you think he'll be gone?" Clare asks.

"Do you need to go? I can take it from here. You've been a big help."

The grin on Clare's face grows even wider. "Hell no, I'm not going anywhere. The real fun begins now that the kid is asleep and can't tattle on us."

"What are you talking about?" I stare at her, perplexed.

"We can snoop around your boss's house," Clare says. "See what we can dig up. You didn't know he had a kid. Clearly, he's keeping secrets. Aren't you the least bit curious? I mean, is Tyler's mother in the picture? Is there a Mrs. Grump?"

I groan and drop onto the sofa in a heap, my head in my hands. "I'm not sure I want to know."

"Well, I want to know," Clare says, and stalks down the hallway. "You're welcome to join me or be the lookout person for when Weston comes home."

I glance at my watch. He's already been gone for over an hour. "He could be back any minute."

"Has he texted you?" Clare asks.

I glance at my phone. "No."

"Well, he said he'd text you when he got news. I don't think he'll be back before he texts you."

Everything inside of me screams that this is a bad idea, but I follow Clare into Weston's bedroom. "Did you do this with Levi?" I ask.

"No, but Levi didn't keep secrets like having a kid from me. If he did, well, we never would have met." Clare quirks a grin and stalks right for the dresser. "Guys always keep the goodies behind the socks or underwear."

"And how would you know that?" I ask.

"Isn't that where you keep your sex toys?"

"No, I keep mine in my nightstand drawer."

Clare bursts out laughing. "You weren't supposed to admit to having sex toys." She grins deviously.

I roll my eyes and grab a pillow off Weston's bed, chucking it at her. "It was just a vibrator. Whatever. Like it's any big deal."

Weston clears his throat behind us. "What the hell is going on?" He stands in the doorjamb, glaring at the two of us.

Clare spins around, slowly trying to ease the dresser drawer closed, but it squeaks, gaining his attention.

She tosses the pillow at me and rushes out of the bedroom. Weston lets her escape. But he blocks the entryway of the door, making sure that I'm not slipping past him.

I fluff the pillow between my hands, using it as a momentary distraction. I could throw it at him, try to dart around him and run back to my apartment.

But I'll have to face him tomorrow at work.

Will he ever let me live this down?

I'm not a coward. But I'm also not ready to be humiliated. Well, it's too late for that, it seems. I place the pillow back onto the mattress like we weren't just snooping through his bedroom.

"Sit," he barks. It comes out like a command, and I obediently do as I'm told.

I plant my bottom at the edge of the bed, and Weston stalks toward me, trapping me between him and the mattress.

"Do you always disrespect the privacy of others?" Weston glares down and I shiver.

"You kept Tyler a secret. What other secrets are you hiding?"

"That's none of your damn business," he snarls, and takes a step back as he paces the length of his bedroom.

I breathe a small sigh of relief when he backs up enough that he's not towering over me, encroaching on my personal space.

Weston loosens his tie and slides it off. Wordlessly, he unbuttons the top button of his dress shirt.

I try not to get turned on by the fact that my boss could very well be stripping in front of me.

Although he showed more skin when he rolled up his sleeves.

He's quiet. But he's not calm. His demeanor is brooding and growing hotter by the second. "What is it that you were looking for?" Weston asks.

I stare up at him, his question catching me off guard. "Hmm?"

"What were you expecting to find?" Weston gestures to the dresser.

I'm honestly not sure. It wasn't even my idea, but I'm not going to blame Clare. I went along with it. I could have stopped her, but I didn't.

"Are you married?" I blurt.

"You tell me, Miss Emerson the detective." He's mocking me. "There are photographs on the walls in the living room. Did you see evidence of a wedding? A wife? A honeymoon?"

"I didn't notice."

He works the cufflinks free on his dress shirt and approaches the dresser. He opens the top drawer, retrieves a small box, and flips the lid, placing the cufflinks inside. "But you found it reasonable to snoop through my bedroom?"

It would be easy to blame Clare. "You never mentioned a kid when we went out on a date." I hate bringing it up, the date from hell. While, as my boss, he might not confide in me that he has a son, I would have hoped that he would have opened up with that when he was dating.

"It was one lousy date, Elisa. My one-night stands don't need to know about my son."

Is that what he wanted that night at the bar? A one-night stand.

"After I left, did you go home with the blonde?" I can't help but feel the bite of jealousy seep into my veins. Why should I care? It shouldn't matter. We're nothing. We never were anything. But it still stings that his attention was on her instead of me.

"What?" he snaps, and shoves the dresser closed. He rolls his sleeves up. His face is red. There's sweat on his brow. The heat has been turned up a little too high, like we're under a heat lamp, baking.

"The blonde you kept eyeing during our date. Did you pick her up? You obviously have a thing for blondes."

He raises an eyebrow. "You think you have me all figured out, Miss Emerson. I assure you that you don't."

"Because you keep secrets," I retort.

"I'm not the only one." Weston approaches the bed, and I want to get up, but I'm frozen inside. "And the fact that I kept Tyler a secret is because no one needs to know about my son. It's no one else's business."

"I don't understand. It's not like you even keep a picture of him in your office."

Weston runs his fingers through his thick dark locks. His hair is messy and wavy. It makes him look even more smoldering and sexy. Damn him.

His jaw is tight, and his gaze is firm on me. The longer he stares, the more I want to reach up and trace the stubble along his jaw. The roughness he exudes goes far beyond his looks.

Instead, I keep my hands planted in my lap, staring up at him, waiting for him to answer.

"I'm guessing that you've never dated a billionaire." He tilts his head, watching my reaction. Is he trying to get a rise out of me?

"I didn't know you were a billionaire," I whisper. He doesn't live the lavish lifestyle of someone who's wealthy beyond measure. He's living in my condominium complex. Who does that?

"I don't make it public knowledge or a habit of telling everyone my secrets," Weston says. He clears his throat. "My son doesn't need to be a pawn in anyone else's game. He doesn't deserve to be photographed and put on display like a wild animal at a zoo."

"No one is suggesting that, Weston," I say. I run my fingers over my pants. My hands are sweaty, but at least he's not berating me for sneaking into his bedroom anymore. The conversation is on him, which I prefer. I want to know everything there is to know about Weston Grump.

"You may not be, but have you seen the headlines with my face as 'Bachelor of the Year'? Like it's a fucking title that I want," he seethes, and leans against the wall. He undoes the black laces of his fancy dress shoes and removes them, one at a time. "I get enough notoriety from my father's company, my company," he says, correcting himself.

His jaw ticks. "I didn't ask for any of this, and the number of women, the moment they realize who I am, they want more than just one night."

"Are you sure that's not because of your wit and charm?"

He glares at me. "I don't need a money-hungry woman searching for a sugar daddy."

"You don't date gold diggers?"

"I don't date," he clarifies, and clears his throat, glancing away. There's a flicker of something, but I can't figure him out.

Is it longing?

Desire?

He certainly doesn't feel that way toward me. And if he did, I would jump out the window. We're a match made in hell.

# SIX

*Weston*

NO ONE WAS SUPPOSED to find out about Tyler. Dammit!

It's not that I'm ashamed of my son, quite the opposite, I want to protect him. And I can't do that if he could be used as a tool against me.

I would give up everything to protect Tyler, and I worry that someone will take advantage of that fact.

Kidnap him.

Hold him for ransom.

And if those fears aren't enough to drive a man mad, the fact that he was born with a rare genetic disorder doesn't help, either.

Not that anyone can tell by looking at him how fragile he is on the inside.

"What do you mean you don't date?" Elisa stares at me longingly, perched at the edge of my mattress.

What the hell was I thinking commanding that she sit on my bed? I should have dragged her out of my bedroom that she was snooping in and sat her on the sofa across from me.

I can't explain the spark I feel when I'm around Elisa. It's magnetic, like an electrical current drawn toward water. She's deadly and dangerous, yet I still keep thinking about her.

When I don't answer her quickly enough, her tongue swipes her bottom lip, and she bites down.

"What the hell were we doing, Weston? When you asked me for drinks?" Elisa asks. She can't just leave it alone.

What I'd give to silence those lips.

I step forward, my legs blocking her from moving, my body trapping her against the bed. I lean down, my thumb guiding her chin up, locking eyes with her. "I thought you'd invite me back to your place."

She scoffs at my words and pulls out of my grasp, knocking me backward as she stands and heads out of my bedroom.

"I'm not just some girl you can fuck," Elisa says.

"We've established that already." I shouldn't have asked her out. It had been stupid, thinking that I could sleep with a girl who lives in the same building. I was hoping for a little booty call every now and then. A friend with benefits type scenario.

And she caught my eye. My cock instantly responded when I saw her, but on our date, she had to be completely different from what I envisioned her to be. That was my mistake.

I'm not proud of having the bachelor status all the damn time.

But I'm not looking for a commitment or relationship. I don't do exclusive. I'm not the kind of man who women want to marry unless it's for my money.

No, thank you.

Elisa grabs her purse from the sofa. "I hope your nanny is all right. I'll see you at work tomorrow."

She heads out the front door, slamming it behind her.

I wince, hoping she didn't wake Tyler.

"Martha is dead," I whisper, not that Elisa can hear a word I'm saying. She's in the hallway, heading for her place.

Tomorrow will be grueling. I can't even fathom how I'm going to deal with Tyler all day. I can't just drop him off at preschool on his day off. He only goes three days per week.

And working from home isn't logistically possible.

I'll have to bring him with me. It's the only thing that makes sense. I lock up the house and shut off the lights. The girls did a decent job of cleaning up the kitchen and dishes. There's not much for me to do other than go to bed.

I check on Tyler, making sure that he's sound asleep before I head to my bedroom. I jump in the shower, hoping it'll cool me off, but all it does is make me think about the girl next door.

Elisa Emerson.

Naked.

Writhing in my arms as I drive my cock deep inside of her trembling body. Her pussy tightening and clenching onto my shaft, taking me with her.

My cool shower becomes hot, and I'm stroking my length, imagining it's her hand, her lips, her pussy surrounding me.

I shouldn't be thinking about her.

It's not only because she's my employee, but fuck, she was a shitty first date. The worst.

Granted, it's not her fault her hair caught on fire. I ought to sue the waitress who forgot to blow out the flaming shot before dropping it into the beer. But it's not like I need the money. And I'm not about to fight Elisa's battles for her.

I finish off in the shower, grab a towel, and head to the bedroom to dry off. My phone pings because someone just sent me a text message.

I approach the nightstand and glance down at my phone. It's from Elisa.

I wipe my hands, making sure they're not wet when I reach for the phone. The towel is dropped and discarded on the floor, forgotten.

Opening the app, I read her message.

*Elisa: Sorry for snooping.*

I click on the screen to type and accidentally swipe the video chat button.

She answers it before I can hang up.

"Are you accepting my apolo—" she doesn't finish her sentence. "Weston, you're naked," she rasps.

The screen doesn't show anything more than my torso, but she's right, I am naked. And I definitely didn't mean to call her while drying off after my hot shower, where I beat off thinking about her.

I cannot catch feelings for Elisa.

I did that once before, and it didn't work out for either of us.

"I'm just in my pajamas," I say. It's a lie, but she can't see anything below my waist.

It's obvious she's blushing. Her cheeks are red, and she glances away from the screen.

Do I make her nervous?

Or is she turned on right now because she's attracted to me?

"Look at me," I say.

She scrunches her nose and shuts her eyes, turning her head to the screen. "Did you put a shirt on yet?"

"No, I told you I'm in my pajamas."

"Wait, you sleep naked?"

I can't help but laugh as I collapse onto the mattress and keep my phone positioned, so she doesn't get a view of anything but my face and chest. "Wouldn't you like to know?"

"No, I wouldn't. I'm sorry I texted," Elisa says.

"Wait." I'm not ready for her to end the call yet.

She raises an eyebrow, interested.

"What was that earlier you were telling Clare about your vibrator?"

Her eyes widen in horror. "Goodnight, Weston!" She ends the call.

I grab a pair of boxers from my dresser and slide them on in case Tyler wakes up in the middle of the night. He's the reason that I don't sleep in the buff.

I'm not tired. There's something about Elisa that makes me not want to shut my eyes and fall asleep. Maybe it's the adrenaline rush of being around her. She makes me feel things I swore off, emotions I vowed never to open up again.

Lying in bed, I download the dating app that Elisa has, curious about all the fuss. I've never been one to date online. I find women in bars, at my apartment complex, rock climbing, wherever I go.

Besides, online means I have to fill out a profile and let people know who I am. I prefer to keep the mystery alive.

I sign up with an account, not that I plan on using it. Having remembered Elisa's username, I type it into the search bar and feel giddy when her picture pops up.

What the hell is wrong with me?

I shouldn't care who she dates. We went out, and it was horrible. Yet I can't stop thinking about her. Clearly, she was good with Tyler, which means a lot to me, the fact that she was kind and decent to my son.

Maybe that shouldn't be asking for a lot, but I don't introduce him to very many people. I keep my work life and my private life separate. Well, I did until Elisa and I became neighbors. That wasn't her fault.

And in a few months, the updates on the house will be finalized, and we can leave the unit we're renting and return home.

I poke through Elisa's dating profile, reading all about her interests, likes, and dislikes.

I scroll through the pictures that she's shared online. The images are of her and her girlfriends, including Clare and Sloane. She's drinking and laughing in one photograph taken outside at a baseball game. In another, she's sitting by the campfire at dusk and on a hike with her friends. There's a picture of her at the beach in a bright red bikini, and damn, does she look good.

But that photo worries me that she'll catch creepers.

In every image, she has a natural smile. The pictures don't look forced. She's having fun and enjoying life.

Before looking at the photos, I wouldn't have taken her for an outdoorsy girl. I want to get to know the real Elisa, behind the walls we've built up around ourselves and each other.

I create a profile. I grab a few pictures that I have from the last time that I was at the beach. I crop off the head, making sure that all anyone can see is my body. There are no discernable marks or tattoos on the photographs to give me away.

I click on her profile, and after I click like, I message her through the dating app. I just have to wait and see if she responds.

If she ever discovers that I'm the man behind the account, I'm not sure she'll forgive me.

———

The next morning, I have no choice but to bring Tyler to work with me. It's not ideal, but I can't ask my driver to watch him.

How much trouble can a three-year-old get into at the office?

Hopefully, not much. I get dressed and make sure that Tyler is ready, with a bag of snacks and toys tossed into a backpack. I carry him into the elevator.

Elisa is already waiting for us when we get downstairs.

"Hey, Tyler," Elisa says, greeting him with a warm smile. "I didn't know you were coming with us today."

"I don't have other nanny arrangements," Weston says, and clears his throat.

"Do you want me to call Clare and ask if she can help watch him?"

"Why would I do that?"

Elisa's bottom lip juts out. She's adorable when she's pouty. "Because she's a nanny, and you clearly need help."

"She's a glorified babysitter. No offense," I say. "A nanny is someone who would live in my home and help with Tyler. I don't want different sitters coming into his life."

"Afraid he'll take after his old man and become a bachelor?" Elisa jokes.

"Old man?" I repeat. Elisa is only a few years younger than I am, not much.

"It's an expression. Relax," she says as we head outside the minute Camden pulls up out front of the building.

Seeing Tyler in my arms, Camden pops the trunk and grabs my son's car seat. I secure it into the vehicle, making sure it's safe before buckling my son inside it. I climb into the front seat, since there's not comfortably enough room for the three of us.

"Everything okay?" Camden asks, glancing at me.

I shake my head. "Martha had a heart attack last night."

"Oh no, that's horrible," Camden says.

"It was definitely shocking," I mutter, and rub my forehead. I barely got any sleep last night, wondering how I was going to handle Tyler on my own.

Martha had been like family, helping me raise Tyler since the moment he came home from the hospital.

Tyler clutches his stuffed animal. He's attached to the blue dinosaur, brings the damn thing everywhere with him, and sleeps with it. Which wouldn't be a problem, but the number of times that we forget it or misplace it makes bedtime atrocious.

Martha had been good with helping remember Roar. That's what Tyler had named his soft blue friend.

Elisa is speaking softly to Tyler, and I swear she's lulling the kid back to sleep. Is it her soothing voice?

Usually, he's a chatterbox at this hour, which requires an extra jolt of caffeine to stay awake.

I glance back at her over my shoulder and she's playing on her phone, since Tyler seems to be asleep.

Is she glancing at the dating app? Has she seen that she has a new match and a new message?

She stares attentively at her phone and glances up when she catches me watching her. "Did you say something?" she asks.

"Just wondering what has you glued to your phone."

"A hot date." There's a smirk on her face, and I can't tell if she's playing with me or if she actually saw the message. I'll have to wait and check if she has replied on the dashboard.

We pull up out front of the office, and I step out, coming around to open the back door to unbuckle Tyler from the car seat.

Elisa has already unbuckled him for me.

I lift him, careful not to hit his head as I carry him inside. He's dead weight and asleep.

Elisa grabs his stuffed animal and hurries after me, catching up when we get inside out of the cold. "Thank you," I say, grateful that she didn't forget his best friend.

"Don't mention it," she says, smiling as she watches him. I swear, if Tyler weren't my kid, I'd be jealous of how much attention she's giving him.

We head up to the elevator, and Tyler squirms, shifting in my arms, beginning to wake up. I rub his back, and Elisa punches the elevator buttons as we head up to my office.

It's too bad there isn't a daycare facility at the office. It's an upgrade that I might consider making in the near future, for Tyler's sake. That way, I can be around my son more while I work and won't have to bring in another nanny to take Martha's place.

I just have to manage the logistics, and I already have enough work to keep me here until ten at night. I choose to leave earlier, meaning that I'm always behind.

I carry Tyler up to my office, and by the time I reach the room and flip on the light, he's decided his cat nap is over.

I put him down on the black leather sofa against the wall along with the backpack, pulling out a handful of toys to occupy him while I'm working.

So much for not letting anyone know I have a kid.

"Is there anything you need?" Elisa asks, staring at me. Her usually pale-blue eyes are bright and warm, sunny. She's asking if my son needs anything, not if I want a pastry, fresh coffee, or romp in my office. Although the last one is out of the question, and not only because Tyler is hanging out with me for the day.

"Actually, I do. Come in and have a seat," I say, and gesture for the chair across from my desk.

"Should I grab a notepad and pen?"

"Yes, please do that," I say, and wait for her to run to her desk, grab what she needs and return. She also brings the blue dinosaur, placing it on the black sofa beside my son.

"Thank you," Tyler says with the biggest smile. His cheeks redden, and he bats his long lashes. I swear I've never seen him give that look to anyone else.

"Martha, the nanny, is no longer with us," I say, refraining from using any more specific terminology like death or heart attack. I don't know how much Tyler understands about that sort of thing, and I'm not ready to have that conversation with him yet. I merely explained to him this morning that Martha wouldn't be coming back but that she loved playing with Tyler very much.

Elisa opens her mouth and quickly shuts it.

She already gathered as much when we drove to work together. Tapping her pen against the pad of paper, she waits for me to give her something that she needs to jot down.

"I want to spend more time with my son, and I think we should open a daycare in the building downstairs. I need you to look into the cost of renting out additional space in the building we're currently in and how many providers we will need on a per child basis according to state law. I also need you to begin to compile several lists. One for a daycare director, to handle the hiring of the teachers. I want to be involved in the final interviews, but I don't need to waste my time on the day-to-day tasks."

Elisa's eyes widen. "This is quite a big undertaking, sir. Would it not be better to find a preschool nearby to enroll Tyler?"

"He is enrolled in a private preschool, but it's three mornings per week. Which means I need someone for the rest of the day or to transport him to another facility like daycare. I want my staff and myself to be able to visit with my son for lunch or check in to make sure that he's doing well."

"I am happy to make phone calls, do research, whatever you need, sir. But I do want you to realize that he's three. In two years, he'll be going to kindergarten—"

Does she think that I'm doing this solely for me? Yes, this is what I want, but I don't intend on shutting down the daycare once Tyler outgrows it. "I know what I'm doing, Elisa."

"Very well, I'll get this information to you as soon as possible."

She hurries out of my office, and Tyler immediately jumps down from the sofa and heads straight out of my office without so much as a word.

"Tyler, what are you doing?"

My son completely ignores me and hurries over to Elisa's desk. I lean sideways in my chair, watching the exchange between them.

Tyler climbs onto her lap. I swear the kid is infatuated with her. He's not the only one.

Damn.

When did I start catching feelings for my assistant? Sure, she's cute. That's why I asked her out for drinks before I knew she worked for me. But our personalities clash.

But a guy can fantasize.

And now that my live-in nanny is gone, it's not like I have an in-house babysitter anymore. It would be cruel to ask Elisa to babysit my son while I went out for an evening. I'm pretty sure she'd kick me in the balls if I even suggest it.

"Tyler, leave Elisa alone," I say. "She has work to do."

"It's all right. I don't mind the company," she says.

I don't believe her. She's just trying to be nice. I stand and head out of my office. I'm not sure how she's able to get her work done, but he seems to be behaving.

"Is he giving you trouble?" I ask, coming around to her desk. I don't want her to be distracted and fall behind because of my son. That isn't fair to her.

"No more than you do on an average day," Elisa quips.

"Nothing about me is average," I say, pinning her with my stare.

She takes in a sharp breath and locks eyes with mine. "Mr. Grump—" she starts, and I cut her off.

"I think we're past that, Miss Emerson," I say, driving home my point. I lean in and ruffle Tyler's hair.

"How about you say goodbye to Elisa, and I let you eat a snack in my office?"

Tyler's eyes light up. He grins and plants his palms on her cheeks and a chaste kiss on her lips.

Elisa is startled, and she's not the only one.

"How many girls has he seen you kiss?" Elisa asks with a nervous laugh as she helps put his feet on the floor. I scoop him up before he can run down the hallway and distract any more colleagues.

"None. I have a strict policy to not bring any dates home."

Elisa stares at me. I swear she's unconvinced, not that it matters. I don't have to prove anything to her. But I still can't believe my son kissed Elisa before I did. How is that even possible?

# SEVEN

*Elisa*

TYLER, Weston's son, is a real charmer. He's a sweetheart, unlike his grumpy dad.

I relinquish Tyler to his father while I focus on getting the new project that Weston wants started, along with the acquisitions work that needs to get done so that we can look at launching several films.

I'm behind on work, and while I could easily stay late and finish everything, then I lose my free ride home, and it's nice to not have to take the subway.

Weston is spoiling me, whether he knows it or not.

While I'm tempted to know about Tyler's mother, I can't downright ask. Certainly not at work. Maybe if we're alone together sometime, which seems unlikely. I could invite him out to lunch, but Tyler would accompany us, and I don't want to ask in front of the little boy.

I spend the day getting as much work as possible done. I also call several different local tailors. I tried on the gown for Clare's wedding, and the black dress is sexy, but it doesn't fit quite right. I need the hem lifted, and the gown pinched in around the breasts.

It shouldn't be overly complicated, and if I knew how to sew, I'd do it myself. But I haven't touched a sewing machine since middle school.

I leave three messages, hoping one of the businesses will call me back.

If not, I'll figure out something. Maybe Sloane knows how to sew and can save my ass?

Nearing the end of the day, I cruise my phone, checking my messages. Nothing from the tailors, but I do have a new message on the dating app.

I open the app and click on the profile of the sender. There's no face, but the guy has a rocking body. He must work out daily. There isn't much about him, and the profile is new.

I open the messages to read the message that he sent.

*Steamy Single Dad: Sunny in Paris, your profile caught my eye. What was it like living in France?*

I hit reply and quickly type a brief response.

*Sunny in Paris: I've never lived in Paris. But it's a place I've always wanted to visit. Will you share any pictures of your face? I'm not into headless dudes.*

I won't keep conversing with him if he doesn't send me a picture that includes his face. I mean, he could have easily sent me a photograph of Thor's body and not his own.

It doesn't show that he's online. Too bad. I stand up and stretch. I've been seated at my desk all day, and my neck is paying the price. I head down the hallway for the breakroom, surprised to find Tyler and Weston grabbing snacks.

"I didn't see you two leave your office," I say, offering a friendly smile to Tyler.

"You were busy on your phone," Weston says.

"Just checking messages. I'm waiting to hear back from the tailor for Clare's wedding."

His gaze flickers. "When is that?"

"Less than ten days."

"Coming up on a tight deadline."

"Tell me about it," I mutter. "I'll figure something out."

Tyler has practically one of every snack out of the vending machine. "You're going to spoil your dinner," Weston says. He lifts him into his arms and glances at the breakroom clock. "Do you want to leave early?"

Is he talking to Tyler or to me?

"Elisa?" he asks.

My cell phone rings. "I need to get that, but yes, I'm done whenever you are." I answer the caller and wander back toward my desk. I'm relieved to find a tailor willing to make the alterations in time for the wedding.

Weston waits by my desk, and the minute I hang up, he's staring at me. "Good news?"

"The best. I just need to pick up my dress and head to Hunts Point. The tailor is in the Bronx."

Weston shakes his head. "You're not going there alone. I'm not sure I even want you going there at all."

"I'll be fine. Don't worry, I'll grab a cab and—"

"No." Weston is firm. "I'm not having you travel into an unsafe neighborhood. Absolutely not."

"What do you suggest I do? No one else is available on such short notice." I run a hand through my hair. "I'm sorry, this isn't your problem. I'll deal with it." I shouldn't be venting at Weston about the dress.

"It's my problem, because you work for me and I'm not going to be out an assistant when you end up dead or sex trafficked."

I laugh at his remark. "Murdered, maybe. But sex trafficked?" I glance down at my curvy body. "You're kidding, right?"

He bites down on his bottom lip, shakes his head, and heads into his office. I don't know what he's doing, packing up his kid's backpack perhaps?

A few minutes later, he reemerges from his office and hands me a business card. I assume it has to do with work. "Do you need me to call him for you?" I ask.

"I already reached out to him, and he will be coming by this evening to your place to have you fitted. Your dress will be ready for the wedding."

"He does house calls?" I ask. That's unheard of. "How much is he, Weston?"

"You can make it up to me with a dance sometime." Weston smirks with a twinkle in his eye.

"A dance? We're not going on another date." Has he lost his mind?

Weston heads into his office to grab Tyler's turtle backpack. "Just say thank you and accept the generous offer of help." He holds his son's hand as the three of us head for the elevator.

I wonder if the rumor mill is going to be filled with all sorts of gossip now that everyone knows Weston has a son. It probably doesn't help that I'm always coming into work and leaving with him in the evening.

We head downstairs and Camden is waiting for us outside by the front entrance. He opens the back door on the driver's side, and I shuffle into the vehicle while Weston helps secure Tyler into the backseat.

"Daddy, where's Roar? Are we going home?" Tyler asks.

Weston unzips the backpack and hands him the blue dinosaur. "Yes, we're heading home and going to make dinner. Do you want to join us?" he asks, glancing at me.

"No, I've got the dress appointment that you made, remember?"

"I can have him meet us at my place. It's no big deal. It's not like it's any farther for him."

I laugh nervously. "Are you asking me out on a date, Weston?"

He snaps the buckle for Tyler's car seat and shuts the door before answering me. The question hangs in the air and my stomach flops as I wonder what he'll say.

Aside from the bad date that we were on together, he's my boss. It's not appropriate to be wining and dining with him, especially in his house.

Weston climbs into the front seat while Camden gets behind the wheel.

I secure my seatbelt and open the dating app, glancing at a new message that popped up sometime this afternoon.

"I'm asking you to dinner, as two friends and colleagues do together," Weston says. "Besides, I owe you a thank you for helping with Tyler last night."

Will he give me an explanation too? Like why his kid was such a secret.

"I can do dinner, but I left the business card on the office desk."

"I'll have the tailor come by my place." Weston calls and makes the adjustments with the meeting location. When he ends the call, he glances back at me. "He said to bring your shoes, if your hemline needs to be tailored to your heels."

"Thanks." I breathe a sigh of relief and glance at the new message from *Steamy Single Dad*.

*Steamy Single Dad: Don't worry, I'm not actually a headless dude.*

There's a picture attached to the message, but his face is blurred out. Seriously? I shouldn't give him the time of day, but I have a few minutes to kill while in the backseat.

*Sunny in Paris: Tease. Sleepy Hollow is about as much interest as I have in headless men. Have any other pics or am I going to block you?*

I hit send and Weston's phone pings a few seconds later.

He glances at his phone, but I can't see what he's looking at. "The tailor texted that he's going to stop for dinner and will be a few minutes late. I told him not to rush. Anytime tonight is fine."

"Thanks."

After we're dropped off at our building, I head inside to change clothes, freshen up, and grab my gown and shoes.

Weston insists to just come on over whenever I'm ready.

I'm not sure that I'll ever be ready for dinner with him. But at least it's not a date. I mean, his kid is with us. That means that it can't be a date. It's just friendly chit chat over a nice meal together.

Not a date.

I grab my dress on the hanger and shoes, stalking next door. I give a firm knock.

"It's open," Weston says.

I try the door handle and, sure enough, he left it unlocked. "You're worried about something happening to me in the Bronx, but you leave the door unlocked?"

Weston is in the kitchen, dicing up ingredients for a salad. He has three bowls out, although one of them is made of plastic and smaller than the other two.

"I'm not doing two funerals in one week," he says pointedly.

I swear the air leaves my lungs.

"Point taken," I say, and slip out of my shoes. I hang my dress on the empty coat hook by the front door. "Can I help?"

"That depends. Do you know how to cook?" Weston asks.

"Daddy, I want carrots," Tyler says, and comes dashing at Weston. He holds out his hand, offering a tiny slice, and the little boy takes it from his father before wandering aimlessly around the kitchen.

"So, is there a Mrs. Grump in the picture?" I ask.

He puts the knife down with a heavy thud on the counter. There's a heat in his eyes. "Do you think I'd have asked you out if I was married?"

"No," I say softly. "I was just curious." I glance at Tyler, not wanting to outright ask where the kid's mother is at.

He must see right through my question. Am I that obvious? "It's just the two of us. Always has been. Always will be," Weston says.

"You're doing a remarkable job with him," I say.

"I do my best." He picks up the knife and resumes chopping up vegetables and lettuce for the salad.

"Daddy." Tyler climbs onto his seat at the table and sits on his knees. "I'm hungry."

Weston prepares the three of us a nice dinner. We open a bottle of wine, killing just about all of it by the time the meal is through.

Afterwards, I help with the dishes while he gets Tyler washed up and ready for bed.

I debate leaving. There's no reason for me to stay, except that the tailor is supposed to come to Weston's place instead of mine. Not that he couldn't be redirected again. But if Weston is tucking Tyler in with a story, I don't want there to be any interruptions.

It isn't long before Nigel, Weston's personal tailor, arrives. I hurry into the bathroom to change into the dress and slip on my shoes to let him hem everything perfectly.

Soft footsteps graze the floor, and I glance over my shoulder as Weston sneaks out of Tyler's bedroom.

"It's good to see you, Nigel."

"Nice to see you too, Weston."

"Thanks for coming on such short notice," Weston says.

"Fancy date for the two of you?" Nigel guesses as he pins my dress.

"Just a wedding," I say.

"What? You two are getting married?" Nigel gasps.

"No," we both say in unison.

I'm grateful that the tailor didn't just stab me with a pin. It's obvious that he's distracted, staring up at me and then Weston. "Well, you could have fooled me by the smoldering looks that you two keep exchanging. Dating?"

"No," I say, this time quicker than Weston can answer.

He finishes the hemline and has me turn around to face Weston.

Weston's dark gaze widens as he stares at the V-neck of my gown, which reveals an ample amount of cleavage.

"You're going to take in the top, right?" Weston asks.

"That's up to Miss Emerson, is it?"

"Yes, and I'd like it well-fitted, but it doesn't have to hide my cleavage. I do have boobs," I say with a laugh.

Weston's ears redden and he glances away.

"Did something I say make you uncomfortable, Weston?" I ask. It's the first time I've seen him look flustered.

He clears his throat and a few seconds pass while he slowly recovers. "Not at all. I'd just hate to see you pop out of your dress."

"And what exactly might pop out?" I ask, staring at him incredulously. I try not to laugh as he shifts on his feet. "We aren't talking about my breasts, are we?" I'm teasing him. I can't help it. I want to see him squirm.

His tongue darts out to the corner of his lip. "I just don't think every man at the wedding needs to see your breasts, Elisa."

"Do you want to see my breasts?"

Nigel is a professional, standing there pinning along the open neckline that dips into my cleavage, revealing an eyeful. He doesn't say a word about the comment that I just made to Weston.

"We're done," Nigel says. "If you'd like to remove the gown, I'll take it with me and have it finished in a few days."

"Thank you," I say, and hurry to the bathroom, closing the door. I change back into my torn jeans and t-shirt. I tried to pick the least sexy outfit I could find on a whim.

Nigel and Weston say their goodbyes and I hand my dress over to Nigel, with his promise that he'll have it back in time for the wedding.

"I should probably head home," I say, pointing at the door.

"Worried about traffic?" Weston jokes. "I know it's quite a distance to your place."

"Very funny." I roll my eyes and walk past Weston, only to feel him grab me by the hips, pulling me against him. He growls and I exhale a nervous breath.

"I like you, a lot," he whispers, his breath teasing mine as he stares from my eyes to my lips.

I don't dare admit that he's grown on me. The burning hate that I felt for him the first day at the office, after our date, it's simmering.

The wine from dinner makes my head spin and the room warm. I lean onto my tiptoes, wanting to kiss him.

"Do you ever wonder what I taste like?" I ask.

A warm smile covers his face. "I have," he admits.

"I've been wanting to taste your lips since that dream I had the other night."

He grabs my hand, not letting me slip out of his reach. "Your lips aren't the only thing that I want to taste. What dream?" The smile grows on his face, wanting to know all of my secrets.

His words send a shiver through me, making me even hotter. "Just a sex dream," I say with a nervous laugh.

"I may need to open a second bottle of wine."

"Are you trying to get me drunk?" I tilt my head, staring up at him, and grimace.

"What's wrong?" He senses my discomfort.

"Kink in my neck," I confess, and hang my head. I want to stare up at him, trace his lips with my tongue, but my body has other ideas, and I don't agree with it.

"Turn around," Weston says, and guides me by my shoulders to face away from him.

I exhale a heavy breath. I'm nervous, my back to Weston. It feels like a vulnerable position, but I trust he wouldn't intentionally hurt me.

His touch is gentle yet firm as his fingers dig into my shoulders, his thumbs grazing along my neck.

A purr escapes my lips; his touch is amazing and electric.

"Did you just purr?" Weston asks with a chuckle.

"No," I lie. He can't prove it. Unless he makes me do it again. And I won't. I'll be more careful how I respond to his touch.

My eyes close and my body begins to relax as he digs into my tight muscles, giving me a neck massage.

"If I knew you were this good with your hands, I'd have requested daily massages as your assistant."

"Oh, sweetheart, I'm good with my hands. This is just the warmup. The preshow." His breath tickles my neck and I shiver from the intensity of his body setting mine aflame.

I lean back and his chest is pressed against my back, steadying me.

With his left hand, he continues to massage my shoulders, and his right trails a soft path up my neck. His touch isn't just calming. It's arousing.

I tug my bottom lip between my teeth. I'm trying not to get turned on by Weston, my boss. We went down this path once; it was a disaster.

And he has a kid. Weston has made it perfectly clear that he just wants sex. And maybe that's all right.

My body certainly agrees.

The room is warm, and I want to undress, strip down and climb atop him, ravish him.

But what if this is just a massage to him? And he doesn't want me?

There's only one way to find out. I spin around in his grasp, his fingers along my neck as I tip my lips up and brush his mouth with mine.

The kiss is soft and gentle at first, almost lazy, like lounging by the fire on a winter's night.

He groans and tugs on my bottom lip, dragging it between his teeth. "Fuck," he growls, lifting me into his arms.

My legs wrap around him, my insides on fire because of the power he exudes. There's a confidence and a sexiness that seeps out of him. Usually, I find him arrogant, but right now I just want to get him undressed.

My fingers deftly work the buttons on his dress shirt free. I take my time, although not intentionally, as my hands tremble.

He takes my hands, bringing them to his lips, kissing my skin. "You can rip it," he says with a smirk.

When I don't tear his shirt open quick enough for his liking, he yanks it open and the buttons pop off, flying across the room.

He puts me down on the kitchen counter. My feet dangle over the edge while he unbuckles his belt and yanks it off.

I press my lips together. "That was hot." Just watching him undress has my body ablaze. I want to feel him, taste him, devour him before the night is through.

Weston unbuttons his dress slacks and pulls down the zipper, stepping out of the expensive material. He tosses it onto a nearby chair. "God, you're so sexy," he whispers, pinning me back against the counter with kisses.

He helps me undress, our lips fused together and only apart a few seconds as my t-shirt crashes to the floor.

Weston's fingers slide into the open tears in my jeans, one of the rips high on my thighs, letting him touch me.

His touch is hypnotic. I stare at his lips, gasping for breath, panting together from the overwhelming intensity building between us.

"I never understood why jeans with rips were fashionable until now," he growls, stroking my inner thigh, his fingers grazing my panties. "Easy access." A wicked grin crosses his features before capturing my lips with his.

Our tongues duel and he lifts me off the counter, carrying me to his bedroom. "Put me down; you're going to hurt your back."

"Sweetheart, even if carrying you did hurt my back, it would totally be worth it." He places me down on the bed, covering my lips with fervent kisses.

Weston trails a path from my collarbone down my neck, his scruff scratching and teasing me as he kisses lower. "There's only one rule in this room," he says.

I stare up at him, breathless. My fingers tease through his hair as I bring his lips back down to mine, both of us wrestling for control.

He growls and pulls back. "Scoot back on the bed farther."

I do as he commands. "Is that your rule? Obey you?" I tease with a smirk.

"You have to be naked," he says, unfastening the button on my jeans. He unzips the denim, his palm grazing over my stomach. His touch is featherlight and sensual, making my body tingle all over. "Hips up."

I do as he says, lifting my hips while he helps shimmy my jeans down my legs and slides them all the way off.

"That's much better. But you're still breaking the rule."

"I am?" I ask, staring up at him, trying to catch my breath, and he hasn't even brought me over the edge yet.

"Naked," he says. His fingers work the clasp of my bra free, sliding the straps down my arms. I let the undergarment fall to a heap on the floor.

My fingers graze across his stomach, my fingers teasing the waistband of his boxers. "Your turn."

Weston shakes his head. "My home. My rules." He keeps me from undressing him and climbs down my torso, his lips and beard grazing over my thighs. His kisses are sweet and warm as he heats me to my core.

"But you're not naked," I whine. He's clad only in his boxers, but I'd rather see him in nothing at all. I want to know what he looks like, feels like, and tastes like.

He presses his lips to mine, drinking me in. Our tongues duel, both of us wanting to take the lead.

In the end, Weston wins, pinning me down, pressing his groin against mine. I can feel his thick, hardened cock, but I want to see it.

"Tit for tat," I say.

Weston raises an eyebrow, and his lips move toward my breast. "I'm all about your tits," he says with a grin before sucking and palming my breast. His tongue moves over my nipple, teasing and kissing me. He blows cool air across the mound where he kissed, watching my nipple harden.

I squirm beneath his touch, desiring more with him.

"I meant both of our panties off," I say, trying to form a coherent sentence.

"Panties? I don't wear panties," he says, correcting me. "But yours can come off." That wicked grin is back, and he helps guide me out of my panties, sliding them down my thighs until I can kick them away.

"Your boxers, Wes."

His eyes flicker and he covers my lips with his mouth, shoving his tongue in, taking what he wants, or rather, needs.

Like an animal is wild, an untamed side is set free and I'm unsure if it's something I said or if he's craving sex as much as I am.

His fingers graze my folds, discovering I'm slick. But he doesn't fuck me. Not yet.

I push at his boxers, but he doesn't help, and his angle makes it difficult for me to remove them. "Off," I say, whimpering when he doesn't let me remove his last article of clothing.

"It's not magic, you can't just command it to disappear. Trust me, I've tried with you, multiple times at the office." He moves closer, bringing his boxers down, letting me see every inch of his cock, throbbing and waiting for attention.

I raise an eyebrow, curious how long he's wanted me. "When?" I ask.

He certainly hasn't acted like it. He's hidden his desires rather well from me.

My fingers graze his shaft, wanting to excite and satisfy him.

I climb onto my knees, gently pushing Weston onto his back as I lean down to take him into my mouth.

His fingers tangle in my hair as I drag my tongue along his shaft. He groans and pulls me back. "Not like this."

"Don't tell me you're a romantic," I say with a chuckle. He doesn't strike me as the kind of guy who wants our first time together to be slow and sensual.

He silences me with kisses, pushing me onto my back, spreading my legs. His fingers tease my folds and he kisses a warm path everywhere except where I want him to kiss me most of all.

He goes slowly, his motions methodical. It's no secret that he's done this before, the way he makes me antsy and my body crave the feel of his cock buried inside me.

But he still doesn't give me what I most of all want. His kisses are on my inner thigh. His stubble grazes my skin and I shift slightly, hoping to get him to rub over my clit.

"Not yet." He smiles knowingly.

I throw my head back with a hearty sigh. "My insides are on fire and you're fanning the flames."

Weston cocks a wicked grin. "That's not all I'm going to do, sweetheart, but I like to give everything I do my full and undivided attention."

I whimper at his words.

He sounds like he's in boss mode.

It's hot.

He's sexy.

And my body is craving release and he hasn't even fucked me yet.

"You're such a tease," I mutter, trying to convince him to satisfy me already.

"Me, darling? You're the one in that dress earlier, with your tits about ready to hang out. Do you know how hard I was with Nigel in the room? I wanted to take you right there on the floor."

"You should have," I say, smiling up at him as he crawls back up my body.

"That's how every good porn movie starts." He chuckles. "But seriously, no. I'm not letting anyone else see you naked. You're mine." He growls and sucks my neck, dropping long, slow kisses, making my insides warm.

"You'd better not leave a mark on my skin," I mutter, prying his lips from my neck.

"And why not? Let the whole office know that you're spoken for," Weston says. He leans down, playfully biting my collarbone. "No more hot dates for you."

"You're evil." I swat his head away from my neck. "I can't have a hickey at the wedding."

"What about three?"

"What?" I gasp and sit up, but Weston pulls me back down against him, tangling our limbs together. "Relax. It's not like you're going to be seated at the singles' table or anything. I'm sure your friends aren't that cruel."

"You don't know them," I say, my jaw dropping. "And Clare is that cruel."

His breath tickles my neck and he trails a soft path of kisses across my breasts and over my navel. "Enough about them," he mutters. "Trust me, it'll be worth it." Fingers roughly caress my skin, marking and claiming me as he delves lower, teasing me before tasting my nectar.

He guides two, then three fingers inside me, stretching me so I can accommodate his size as his thumb circles my clit.

My lips crash against his, my insides clenching down on him, wanting it to be his cock nestled inside of me.

I squeeze my eyes shut and bite down on my bottom lip.

"Look at me," Weston commands.

Slowly, I open my eyes, struggling to stare into his dark, heated gaze. His fingers bring me over the edge as his lips silence me, keeping me from waking his son in the next room over.

I gasp for breath, back arching, toes curling while Weston brings me toward oblivion. My heart pounds wildly, slamming against my chest, trying to break free from its cage.

I collapse against the mattress, and he climbs atop, a huge grin on his face. "My turn, sweetheart, but I promise we're not done with you, either."

He teases the head of his cock against my slickness and my body is already responding to him, to the heat between us, and the uncontrollable fire burning.

Weston inches inside me, going slowly as he fills me and stretches me. He moves his hips down, rocking against me, making my body respond before it's ready.

My fingers rake against his back and down to his hips, wanting to memorize every detail. He's gorgeous, fierce, and I can't comprehend how we got here tonight.

He leans down, his gaze on me, his eyes staring straight into my soul, our existence becoming one.

I wrap my legs around him, pulling Weston deeper, wanting to bring him over the edge with me this time.

"Do you trust me?" he asks.

"Yes," I whisper, staring up at him, and gasp when I realize we haven't opened a condom. I push a hand between us, stopping him. "Stop. Wait."

He pulls back like I burned him, his brow tight, and a stormy look in his eyes.

"We should be using a condom," I say. I can't believe what just happened.

"Shit," he curses. His brow pinches as he rolls to the other side of the mattress, opening the nightstand. He grabs the foil packet and rips it open.

"It's fine, I'm clean," I say, staring up at him.

"Me too," Weston says. "I also can't get a girl pregnant. I wasn't even thinking about protection. I'm sorry."

I don't ask him what he meant. "It's fine," I say, bringing my hand to his cheek, my lips to his. "It was an accident. It's not like we planned this tonight. Right?"

Weston grins. "I totally planned for you to come over and have dinner at my place. Then after, I'd ravish you until the early hours of the morning." He pulls me down to the mattress, pinning me beneath him.

"Liar," I say, laughing and smiling up at him. "I don't believe you."

"Yeah, me either." He guides his cock back inside me, and this time it feels completely natural, like we're meant to be and fit perfectly.

His lips cover mine, our breathing labored. My heart pounds wildly, my toes curling, and I cling to Weston as though my life depends on it for survival as I chase my orgasm. He's right there with me, both of us falling into oblivion.

Sweat coats my forehead, and he rolls off, gasping for air. My skin is slick and I want to curl up against him, but I'm also too exhausted to move.

He climbs out of bed, tosses the condom in the bathroom trash, and shuts off the lamp beside the bed, collapsing on the mattress beside me.

Should I go back to my place? I don't want to overstay my welcome. He hasn't exactly invited me to stay the night.

My legs refuse to move.

Weston wraps an arm around my waist, burying his face in my neck. "Sleep," he says, reading my thoughts.

I do as he says, letting slumber take hold as I drift off to sleep. It's the most peaceful slumber I've had in ages, wrapped in his embrace.

I roll over and the bed beside me is empty. The morning light shines through the sheer curtains, forcing me to cover my face with my hand.

The shower is running.

Weston must be getting ready for work. I force my eyes open, and the clock reminds me that I need to get dressed and be ready shortly.

I climb out of bed, retrieve my clothes, shoes, and sneak out of his place.

What the hell happened last night?

I mean, I remember what happened. I wasn't that drunk, but I slept with my boss, Weston Grump. I hurry into the shower at my house, rinsing last night away, letting it swirl down the drain as I get ready to face a new day.

But how am I going to face *him*?

I've never had a one-night stand. And Weston is, well, Mr. Grump. The man has never indicated that he wants more from me or anyone else.

I'll chalk it up to having too much wine and avoid any discussion on the subject. I can't imagine that he's going to want to talk about it, either.

Finishing in the shower, I dress in a dark-red, knee-length skirt and black shirt, with matching red along the hem. I grab a tube of matching lipstick and apply it before heading out the door.

I slip on the heels that I plan on wearing to the wedding with the outfit that I'm wearing to work. One last glance in the mirror and I smirk, quite pleased.

My phone is completely dead, so I grab a charging cable. I'll need to plug it in while I'm at the office today.

I head for the door, then the elevator, descend downstairs. Weston isn't down here yet and neither is his driver, Camden.

I shift nervously on my heels. Am I overdressed for the office? My stomach flutters and I glance at the elevator as it descends to the lobby.

There's still no sign of Weston.

Did he send me a message that he's running late? I won't know until I can plug in my cell phone and get enough of a charge to read any texts.

I should probably get the battery replaced. My phone isn't that old, but it barely makes it through the day before it requires charging.

Still no sign of Weston or his driver.

Did he leave without me this morning? I didn't think I was running late, but after standing around the lobby for the past twenty minutes, I definitely will be pressed to make it into work on time.

I hurry outside into the frigid winter air and make my way for the subway. The ground is slick with ice and wearing heels was not in my best interest.

My feet are numb, my legs frozen from the short skirt. I thought I'd be nestled inside the back of a heated car on my ride to work.

Sleeping with Weston was apparently a mistake.

I grumble and hurry to the subway, trying to catch the train on time.

I don't make it. The train whizzes past before I'm even down the platform. "Dammit!" I curse and slow down. I don't need to roll my ankle or fall down the stairs. I'm not making it to work on time.

Eventually, I stroll into the office, late. The next train was delayed and then we sat on the tracks for a while. Just my luck.

I head for my desk and glance up at Weston's office. It's dark. The door is open, but he's not inside.

I plug my cell phone in and wait for it to gain enough of a charge that I can power the device on. There are no messages on my desk phone.

I grab a seat at my desk, check my work emails, and get started. I have a feeling that it's going to be a long and tiresome day, especially when I run into Weston.

Where the hell is he, and why isn't he at work?

Is he avoiding me?

Did he go straight to HR to confess what we did last night?

# EIGHT

*Weston*

I'M NOT sure where Elisa and I stand after what transpired last night. I left her in bed, letting her sleep a few extra minutes while I showered and dressed for work.

But by the time I stepped out of the shower, towel wrapped around my waist, she was gone.

Was it too much to hope that she might have snuck into the shower and told me goodbye?

It's wishful thinking and a bit insane, since I don't want a girlfriend. I'm not sure what I even want with Elisa.

Don't get me wrong, last night was amazing. I would love another replay without the massive amount of wine to get us into the mood. My head is a bit foggy with a dull ache. Nothing that a couple of aspirin can't cure.

There's a loud thud from across the hall and I race out of the bedroom to see what the hell happened.

Elisa is nowhere in sight.

Tyler's screams of pain radiate through the house, growing louder and more pronounced.

"Fuck." I hurry to the bedroom. He's on the floor. I don't know how he got down there. He can't magically roll out of bed. The entire reason that I bought the race-car bed was to make sure he was safe.

His screams grow louder and more pronounced. "Come on, let's get you checked out." I lift him into my arms, the cries not settling as I bring him into my bedroom and put him on the mattress.

"Daddy!" he wails the minute that he's not in my arms. It's hard to tell if the pain is that bad or it's the emotional fall that hurt him worse.

But he's not like other kids. Tyler is a ticking timebomb. Any injuries, even mild, in most instances could be devastating for him.

I quickly throw on a pair of jeans and a t-shirt, slipping on my shoes before hurrying out the front door. I head downstairs, relieved that Camden is already waiting. If he wasn't, I'd have grabbed a cab.

Camden glances me over but doesn't say anything about my attire. "Mountain Sinai Kravis Children's Hospital," I say, needing him to get us there right away.

"Are you sure you don't want an ambulance or helicopter ride?" Camden asks.

I'm doing what I can to not scare Tyler as much as possible. The last time we took an ambulance, about six months ago, afterwards he cried every time he saw one on the road or heard sirens. Hysterical, inconsolable sobs.

It's heartbreaking to watch and not be able to do anything to help.

I cradle Tyler in the backseat, keeping him to my chest. "It's okay, buddy, we're going to make sure everything is fine."

My voice cracks and I can't help but worry that he's just like Wren, fragile. A bump on the playground could be fatal.

Camden pulls up out front of the emergency room and I rush Tyler inside, carrying him to the main desk. "My son, he has Vascular Ehlers-Danlos Syndrome. He fell and I need someone to examine him."

Tyler and I are rushed straight back, and he's placed on a gurney and examined while I give them his full medical history.

He's poked and prodded with a number of tests and medical imaging to ensure there's nothing fatal from the fall.

The doctor speaks to us, assures me that he's fine. He will probably have extensive bruising from the injury, but luckily, there were no internal ruptures or tears.

Relief floods through me and my eyes water, but I swallow back the emotion. We got lucky this time. Next time, we might not be.

Shit. I left my phone in the car. I carry Tyler, who is dead weight and sound asleep after the extensive tests, toward the exit.

Camden is seated in the waiting room cruising through his phone. He glances up, a look of relief flooding his features. I feel the exact same way.

"Let me pull up the car," Camden says. He hurries out of the waiting room, and I head to the exit. I wait on the opposite side of the double doors where it's warm and winter isn't assaulting anyone.

In a matter of minutes, Camden pulls up the car. It's not quite as warm as it usually is, but he waited, which is a relief, since I don't have my phone.

"Where to, boss?" Camden asks. "The office?"

"No, take us home."

I don't bother going into the office. I'm not dressed for it and Tyler is my main focus. He is my priority. It was always about keeping him safe. That's why I hired a nanny who had extensive knowledge about his condition and with a medical background as a nurse practitioner.

I check my phone; there are no messages. I don't hear from Elisa. I'm not sure what I was expecting from last night.

I sure as hell didn't plan on sleeping with her. I grab my phone to text her, but I'm not sure what I'll say. Last night was fun? Want to do it again sometime?

The truth is that I need to focus on Tyler.

Elisa is a distraction. A gorgeous one at that, but I can't be thinking about her. She works for me, and I don't need HR telling me that I'm out of line and it's a lawsuit waiting to happen.

Not that I think Elisa would be after my money, but she knows I'm wealthy.

I spend the rest of the day relaxing on the sofa with Tyler, watching cartoons and kids' films that he loves to view on repeat.

There's a knock at the door. "Stay right here," I say, giving Tyler a kiss on the cheek before moving from the sofa to the front door.

I glance through the peephole.

Elisa Emerson.

I open the door, not exactly inviting her inside. "Did you forget something?" I ask, glancing around the place. I hadn't found anything of hers left behind, but I wasn't checking for it, either.

Her mouth drops and she shakes her head. "You weren't at work today. You missed an important meeting with the production company. They flew in to finalize the Brooke project."

"I was busy." I don't elaborate. I stand with one hand on the door and the other the wall, keeping my distance with her. "Something came up."

"I see," she says, and her brow pinches. "This isn't because of what happened last night between us, is it? If I'm the issue, Weston, I'll quit. I told you that from day one."

I exhale a throaty laugh. "I'm not asking you to quit. You do a great job with the acquisitions department and as my assistant."

"But?" she asks, waiting for me to elaborate.

My cell phone rings, and I swear I don't know who it is, but even if it's a telemarketer, I'll be pleased to talk to them right now. "But nothing. I have to take this call," I say, and grab my phone from the counter.

"Will you be at work tomorrow?" Elisa asks. "The staff was wondering why you didn't come in when you had meetings scheduled all day."

"I had an emergency." I shut the door and answer the caller. "What?" I bark.

"Nice to talk to you too," Logan says.

I rub my forehead. "Fuck, sorry."

"Is it a bad time? I can call back?" Logan asks.

No time is ever good, it feels like. "No, it's fine." I lock the front door and grab a seat on the recliner across from Tyler. He's enthralled with his cartoons, which gives me a few minutes to unload on one of my closest friends, Logan Henderson.

"So, Julianna and I are coming up for Levi's wedding," Logan says. "And I, uh, may be bringing a hot date."

His daughter, Julianna, is fifteen, almost sixteen. I still remember the day that kid was born. When the hell did I get so damn old?

"What?" I laugh and cover my hand over my mouth. "You have a date? Dammit, am I the only one of us who is going to be left at the singles' table?"

"Sounds like your love life sucks," Logan quips. "Funny, since you always have a girl on your arm everywhere we go."

"I like to play the field a bit," I say, and shrug. I spend more time focusing on Tyler than anyone else. How am I supposed to find the time for a relationship?

"Whatever makes you happy," Logan says. "Anyways, I met this rockstar of a girl. She's a vlogger and her name is Cali."

I can't help but laugh. "What is she, seventeen?"

"She's legal, Jackass," Logan throws at me. "Twenty-nine, but age is just a number."

"Damn, good for you." I whistle at the fact that he caught a girl fourteen years younger than he is. "Lucky bastard."

Logan laughs. "The girl is anything but lucky. She's cute, though, and sassy. Oh my gosh, the mouth on her. But anyways, we're going to rent a room at the Luxenberg for the wedding. We should catch up, grab drinks while I'm in town."

"That sounds nice," I say, and let out an enormous sigh.

"What is it?" Logan and I served in the military together. The man knows how to read me, which is sometimes good and other times concerning as hell.

"I just, I need to find someone who can look after Tyler. I can't exactly take a three-year-old to the bar and the nanny is, uh, not a possibility."

"Did she quit on you?" Logan asks with a laugh.

"No, she died, you asshole."

"Sorry," Logan apologizes. "Wasn't she like super old?"

"No, she was in her sixties."

There's silence that follows. "I could ask Julianna to watch Tyler while we go out."

I inhale a long, slow breath. "I don't know. I appreciate the offer, but Tyler is special. You know?"

"Unless you're planning on wrapping that kid in bubble wrap, you have to accept that there are some things you can't control. He's got to grow up and live his life. Not have a helicopter parent chasing him around like his shadow."

I pinch the bridge of my nose. "I don't need a lecture from you," I say. He doesn't know what it's like to raise a kid who could die. And at some point, will die, probably before I do. The life expectancy is around forty, which seems far away, but Wren died in her twenties, and she struggled all through her childhood with complications and health issues.

"I get it, you're going through something none of us ever had to deal with," Logan says empathetically. "We commend you for stepping up and being there for Tyler. But he needs room to grow, both emotionally and physically. Don't smother him to death."

I don't so much as feign a smile. "That's not funny."

"Do you want me to ask Julianna to babysit or not?" Logan quips.

"Yeah, you may as well mention it to her. And what's this about you bringing a date? Who's the unlucky girl who got stuck with you?"

"Her name is Cali," Logan says again, "and we met when she came to my resort to do a review on the place."

My jaw drops as I remember the scathing review that had been all over social media about Blue Sky Resort. "You're dating that traitor?"

"Well, her boss is the one who changed the review and tried to destroy the place."

"Wow, vicious." I can't believe he ended up dating the girl after all that drama.

"Cali is actually quite sweet. You'll like her."

"So, who is running the resort while you're in New York for the wedding?" I ask.

"Wyatt."

"Your brother?" I cover my face with my hand, trying not to laugh. "He does realize that he can't sleep with all the guests." Wyatt and I have quite a bit in common. Neither of us have the urge to settle down and start a family.

"I've already told him, repeatedly." Logan chuckles. "Far be it for him to listen to me, but at least he stays away from Cali."

We share a few stories before hanging up, and I work on preparing dinner.

My phone pings with a notification alert and I glance at it, realizing it's a new message in the dating app. I ignore it, finishing with dinner and getting Tyler changed and ready for bed.

He doesn't want to sleep in his race-car bed again after today's spill. I'm not sure that I didn't make it worse, dragging him across town to the hospital for a million different tests.

I put him in my bed, surrounded by pillows, and add a few more pillows to the floor. He's not a kid who usually rolls out of bed, he hasn't done that in well over a year, so I'm not sure what's up with it.

Did he try to get up out of the race-car bed and trip? We've all been disoriented at some point when waking up. But most of us don't have to worry about it killing us.

After Tyler is asleep, I lounge on the sofa, flipping through the channels. There's not much on, nothing new to watch.

My phone pings again, notifying me of another new message.

I grab it from the coffee table and open the dating app. I have two new messages, both are from *Sunny in Paris*.

*Sunny in Paris: Are all men jerks?*

I toss my head back and shut my eyes.

Fuck, I screwed up with Elisa. Royally. I'm not sure what I was expecting or hoping for, especially when she came to my front door.

But this text to *Steamy Single Dad* isn't it. She's mad at me and she's not wrong. I blew her off. I had a shitty day and didn't want to talk about it with her.

She sent me a second message and I scroll down to read it.

*Sunny in Paris: Picture or bust. I'm blocking you if you don't send a photo of you.*

Yeah, that isn't going to help. I can't let her know it's me, and if I grab some random photo off the internet, she can easily do a reverse image search. I don't want to be that shitty guy.

So, I do the next best thing. I open my phone, scroll through my photos until I find one of my buddy, Logan. I'll pretend to be him. At least with the picture. The rest is all me.

And no one has to know.

I upload the photograph of him outside by the campfire. I'm also in the photo but I crop myself out and send it to her.

*Steamy Single Dad: Not all men are jerks.*

I click on her profile and flip through her pictures. Why the hell am I hooked on her? A notification pops up that she's online. She's probably reading the message I sent and looking at the photo right now.

The odds of her knowing Logan are slim. He used to live in New York, but he's been in Montana for a while, getting settled with the new resort that he invested in. While he's also a billionaire, he hasn't been in the media. He's done well to keep most of his private life under the radar.

Breckenridge, Montana. I still can't believe he calls that place home, after living in New York.

Some days, I consider doing something similar. Leaving everything behind and moving to the beach, enjoying all that life has to offer. But I'd worry I'd get bored if I retired early. Besides, there are too many people counting on Blazing Media. They have jobs and lives, and I can't just walk away because I want to. That would be selfish.

A notification pops up that I have a new message. I double click on it.

*Sunny in Paris: Cute, but is that really you? Send another pic.*

I quirk a smile. She's smart. I flip through a few more pictures and land on another one with Logan. I have to crop out his teenage daughter sitting next to him and zoom in, making it more of a portrait.

*Steamy Single Dad: Trust issues, much? Sending now.*

I hit send and attach the image of Logan. I feel dirty, and while I know it's wrong, I want to chat with Elisa, get to know the real her. And I can't do that with both of our walls up. Being her boss is a bit of a cock blocker.

*Sunny in Paris: Wow. Okay, so two for two. Have a third?*

I attach one more photograph of Logan, this one has him snowboarding down the slopes. He's wearing a helmet and gear, so you can't tell it's him, but it's a third photo that I have handy.

*Steamy Single Dad: I've proven who I am. Now it's your turn, Sunny in Paris.*

I click send, along with the picture, and wait for her to respond. I stretch out on the sofa, getting comfortable. While I'm waiting for her to respond in the app, I open my texts and message Elisa.

*Weston: I really hope you don't quit. I'm sorry about this morning, I had an emergency and left my phone behind.*

*Elisa: Emergency? What happened?*

I don't want to get into the specifics with her about Tyler.

*Weston: Everything is fine.*

*Elisa: Everything isn't fine. We need to talk.*

I groan at the message that she sent. Nothing good ever comes from the phrase *we need to talk.*

I don't text her back, waiting to see if she responds to *Steamy Single Dad* although it's probably not a great sign if she does, because that means she's over whatever it is that we shared last night.

My phone buzzes with another message.

*Elisa: Can I come over?*

I tap my fingers over my thighs, debating on if it's wise to let her back into my place. Inviting her over is what complicated things between us. But sitting here and texting her in the dating app, pretending to be someone else, that isn't fair to her, either.

*Weston: Yes, I'll open the door, but Tyler is asleep, so we have to keep it down.*

I stand and flip the deadbolt, allowing Elisa to enter when she's ready to join me.

She doesn't text me back. Two minutes later, she quietly opens the door to the condo and steps inside.

Elisa glances around the house. I'm not sure what she's looking for. I already told her Tyler is asleep. "Can I come in?"

"Sure, have a seat." I gesture to the sofa and fall into the cushions beside her. I could sit on the recliner, alone, but I'd rather be in her proximity. I can't explain it, but being around Elisa, I feel quite a bit calmer and more relaxed.

"About last night," Elisa says, and rests her hands together in her lap. "It was a one-off occurrence. It can't ever happen again." Her face is stoic, and I nod slowly.

"If that's what you want," I say, not telling her how I feel about last night.

"You're my boss. I don't think we should be sleeping together. If anyone at work finds out—"

"They won't," I assure her. "No one will know."

She exhales a nervous breath. Elisa fidgets with her hands in her lap. "Okay, good. I don't want rumors swirling." Her gaze locks on mine. "I haven't told anyone about us."

"Me either," I say. Even if I wanted to, I hadn't had time, since I'd been looking after Tyler all day. "Do you want a beer from the fridge?"

"No, I had more than enough alcohol for the week, yesterday."

Does she regret sleeping with me? I don't dare ask a question that I won't like the answer to.

I lean back in the sofa, letting the cushions envelop me. "So, we'll chalk it up to too much wine and poor judgment."

Her brow tightens and she purses her lips. "Whatever you want to call it, but it won't happen again. It was a mistake."

Elisa's words cut me like a knife, slashing at my chest, causing fresh wounds.

"A mistake?" I really wish I'd have grabbed that beer to distract me. Something to put my lips around as I stare at her features, my gaze traveling down from her nose to her ruby lips.

"We had too much to drink and let our inhibitions down. It happens. Blame it on the alcohol," Elisa says. She stands and folds her arms across her chest. "I'm not upset. I mean, I was when you weren't at the office and I thought you were avoiding me after bailing on my ride to work. But I get it. You had an emergency." She shrugs like she's trying to be cool about the fact I blew her off.

"I had to take Tyler to the emergency room," I say. I wring my hands together. It would be nice if I could have a normal life, but my life is far from it, raising my son.

"What?" Elisa's eyes widen. "Is he all right?"

"He's fine," I say. Her stare is making me nervous. I stand and head for the fridge, opting for that beer after all.

But I'm only having one drink tonight. We can't have a repeat performance of last night. Especially since my little guy is sound asleep in my bed.

She nods slowly, watching me. "That's a relief. So, we're good?"

"When weren't we good?" I chuck back, popping the lid off the beer bottle.

"I wasn't sure. You kind of slammed the door in my face rather abruptly, Wes."

I inhale sharply at the nickname and her brow furrows, noticing my reaction. I try to hide it. Pretend that it doesn't bother me, because there was only one person in the world who ever called me *Wes* and she's dead.

"I had an important phone call," I say, trying to shrug off what happened. "I'm sorry if it came across as rude or abrupt." I am truly sorry for hurting her feelings, that wasn't part of my plan and isn't who I am. I don't do things to hurt someone I care about.

"Apology accepted," Elisa says. "I'm glad we're back to being friends."

"Do you want to stay, watch a movie or something?" I offer.

"As friends?" She raises an eyebrow, like she's making sure this isn't a proposition that will lead to something else. Is it the end of the world if it did? "Because I can't be sleeping with my boss."

"Got it. You want to stay for a movie or not?" I ask, taking another swig from my beer.

She purses her lips, thinking it over. "Do you have popcorn?"

We watch a chick flick that she picks out and I'm beginning to wonder why I agreed to it. It's not like I get the benefit of sleeping with her at the end of the night, subjecting myself to a rom-com that is entirely too flirty and too unrealistic. Love isn't that sweet. It would be ninety minutes of torture if I didn't have the luxury of glancing at Elisa every so often.

Her laugh.

Her smile.

The way she darts her tongue out and it touches the corner of her lips.

When the hell did I become so damn smitten over a girl?

After the movie ends, I shut off the television and toss the empty popcorn kernels from the bowl into the garbage.

"Do I have a ride to work tomorrow or are you not going to make it into the office?" Elisa asks.

"Camden will drive us into work in the morning. Don't be late."

"I wasn't late this morning," Elisa says.

She heads across the hall, back to her place, and I lock up the apartment.

Already, I miss her company. It was nice having an adult to converse with, someone who isn't babbling on about his favorite cartoon character and can he watch another episode before bed.

I close up for the night, shutting off the lights and heading to my bedroom when my phone pings.

It's a notification from *Sunny in Paris*.

I open the dating app and read her newest message.

*Sunny in Paris: You're cute, but why are you still single? What's the catch?*

I hit reply and begin to type my message.

*Steamy Single Dad: No catch. I have a son. It doesn't give me a lot of time to meet women.*

I put my phone down on the dresser and lift Tyler into my arms, carrying him back into his bedroom, putting him in bed.

If he freaks out tomorrow again with the race-car bed, I'll donate it and get him a new frame or put the mattress on the floor.

Closing the door to his bedroom, I head back to my room and there's already a message waiting from *Sunny in Paris.*

*Sunny in Paris: I can understand that. Can't bring a child to a bar. How old is he?*

She asks a lot of questions but hasn't really given me anything about her. I slip out of my jeans and climb under the covers, messaging her back.

*Steamy Single Dad: He's young, under five.*

I don't want to give too much away or for her to suspect that I'm the man she's conversing with, but I don't think at this point she has any idea.

I continue my message to her.

*Steamy Single Dad: You still haven't told me why you're still single. A beautiful woman like yourself, I'm sure that you get asked out all the time.*

I turn the bedside lamp off but continue looking at the screen. She's online, so I wait for her to message me back. In a matter of minutes, it pings.

*Sunny in Paris: I'm not always great at picking out the best men.*

I quirk a grin. Is she talking about me?

*Steamy Single Dad: Elaborate.* I respond and wait for her to answer.

*Sunny in Paris: I went out with my boss.*

Now, it's getting juicy. I sit up, grabbing a few pillows to prop myself up.

*Steamy Single Dad: And is he hot?*

*Sunny in Paris: That's not the point. He's my boss.*

Well, we did more than going out, unless she's referring to the first time that we met and I don't think that she is. That feels like ancient history after what happened last night between us.

*Steamy Single Dad: Well, I mean it's probably no big deal unless you slept with him.*

I can't believe I hit send on that message, but hell, I'm having way too much fun. It's like being one of her girlfriends and getting the lowdown on the night she spent over at some guy's house.

*Sunny in Paris: I don't usually do that. And I can't believe I'm telling you this because I will NEVER do that again. I'm not a one-night stand kind of girl. Never have been and never will again. Just. No. So, if you're hoping that I'll be a hookup, you can chat with someone else.*

At least she's making her point loud and clear.

*Steamy Single Dad: I'm not interested in a hookup, Sunny in Paris.*

It takes her a few minutes to respond, and I begin to wonder if she fell asleep. It is getting late. My phone pings, alerting me that she answered.

*Sunny in Paris: Good, because most guys lose interest after the third date if sex isn't on the table.*

Wow, so she really does like to take things slow. I commend her for it. While it's not something that I'm used to doing, I have no issue with how other people live their life.

*Steamy Single Dad: I'm not like most guys.*

Yeah, because I usually get lucky on the first night. But I refrain from mentioning that to her.

*Sunny in Paris: Are you willing to meet up for coffee?*

I exhale a heavy sigh. I didn't think this through. Of course she'd want to meet or chat on the phone. Maybe even video call to make sure I'm who I say I am. The jig is up.

When I don't answer her fast enough, she replies.

*Sunny in Paris: I prefer to meet the person I'm chatting with online early on, to make sure they're who they say and there's chemistry. I've been on one too many bad dates and I'd like to meet you.*

We've both had a string of bad dates, our most recent being with each other. At least mine was, and I assume her last date was with me. But who knows. If she's messaging me on the app, how many other guys is she talking with?

I hadn't actually deleted any new messages when I teased her that day at the office, stealing her phone from her. I was trying to flirt with her.

It was a dangerous move and could have backfired.

Yeah, so could this, pretending to be Logan while chatting with my assistant.

I don't answer her message. I leave her hanging, sign off from the app, plug my phone in and roll over for bed.

But my dreams are filled with Elisa, her womanly curves, bright eyes, and wicked grin. And they're not sweet dreams, either. I'm nipping her skin, biting and leaving marks, devouring her as she screams my name over and over again.

I wake up in a sheen of sweat. Not once. Not twice. But four times. I swear the dream version of Elisa is going to kill me.

In the early hours of the morning, I shower under a steamy spray, letting my filthy and vivid thoughts of her sucking my cock fuel me as I stroke my shaft.

She's all I think about, envision, as I finally let go.

Shit.

It was bad enough, her getting in my head before we had sex. But now that I've had her in my bed, she's constantly in my mind. All I can think about.

She's like an addiction and I'm craving my next hit.

I finish showering just as the sun begins to rise. I get dressed and put on a pot of coffee while I wake Tyler and get him out of his pajamas and ready for work with me.

He missed preschool yesterday while he was at the hospital having tests run. Not that I could have dropped him off and picked him up. I could request that Camden handle chauffeuring Tyler around, but he shouldn't be responsible for my son. That's what Martha had been there for, to help with my boy.

I should hire a new nanny, someone to give Tyler undivided attention instead of focusing on starting a daycare center in the building. And while I could do both, my time is running short as it is with trying to get my job done on a limited work schedule.

When my father was alive and I worked from home, I'd put in long days and late nights. I swore that I wouldn't do that after he passed, that I would set boundaries and a healthy work schedule. But it's difficult to get everything done before the end of the day.

And adding on more responsibilities, like finding Tyler a new nanny or creating the daycare in the building, aren't small projects to tackle. It's like adding another mountain of work to do when I already have Everest to climb.

Tyler and I head downstairs, and Elisa is waiting for us in the lobby. "Good morning," she says as we approach.

Camden is already waiting, and we shuffle outside and into the cold like we had days ago, as if nothing happened between us.

I'm grateful for the chance to start fresh with Elisa. Even if she doesn't see me as someone worth dating, I don't want to be remembered and hated as the man she fell into bed with while drunk.

I don't want to be her biggest regret.

We head to the office, and I get Tyler situated on the sofa playing with his action figures. He's not particularly quiet but I can handle his noise level. At least he's having fun and doesn't seem to mind being stuck with me all day.

"Sir," Elisa says as she knocks on my open office door.

I'm on the phone with one of our lawyers. The film we had a green light to finance, it turns out had more than one screenplay and we weren't made aware of it. Someone else is trying to steal the script out from under us to produce before we get it to launch.

I gesture her to come on in.

Elisa takes a seat across from me as I speak heatedly with Gary, our media lawyer. I'm trying to watch my words, since my son is in the office. And while he doesn't appear to be paying much attention, the kid is an absolute sponge at this age.

I finally hang up, slamming the phone down.

"Bad time to ask if you want anything for lunch?" Elisa quips.

I glance at my watch. I hadn't realized it was nearly one o'clock. I've been powering through as much as I can, and while I have a great staff who helps, we're short-handed, since a number of them quit weeks ago when I took over.

"I need a break," I say, and stand, stretching. "Tyler, do you want to go out to lunch?"

"Yes, Daddy!" Tyler squeals and drops his dinosaur action figures onto the floor. He jumps off the sofa and I grimace, terrified my son is going to fall and get hurt.

"Tyler!" I can't help but scold him. "You have to be careful."

It's hard for him to grasp what can happen if there's any trauma to his body. At three, he doesn't have the understanding that even a bump on the playground could be fatal.

"He's fine," Elisa says, and Tyler takes her hand.

She stares at me like I've lost my mind. She has no idea what we've been through as a family. "He's not fine. If he falls or bumps into something aggressively, he's at risk of rupturing his internal organs."

"What are you talking about?" Elisa asks, glancing down at Tyler. She gives him a warm, friendly smile. "Grab your stuffed dinosaur. I'm going to talk to your daddy out in the hallway."

She grabs my arm, practically dragging me out of my office.

"What the hell are you talking about, Wes?"

I exhale a shaky breath. "Tyler has Vascular EDS, just like his mother."

"I don't know what that is," Elisa says, shaking her head, waiting for me to elaborate.

"He has a collagen deficiency that puts him at risk of rupturing his internal organs and arteries."

"I've never ..." She pauses, trying to speak. "I didn't know, I'm sorry. I'm sure you're just trying to protect him. I didn't realize that he... Is he going to die?"

I exhale a heavy breath. "I intend on protecting him as long as I can, but life expectancy is forty. However, my sister barely made it into her twenties. Wren constantly had health issues related to her diagnosis. She had multiple surgeries and complications all throughout her childhood and teens."

"That's awful, I'm sorry. I had no idea."

The way she looks at me. "I don't want your pity. You asked and I thought I should explain why I'm forceful when it comes to his safety. It's why having a nanny who knew about his condition was so important to me."

Elisa opens her mouth. "You let me watch him. I had no idea..." her voice trails off.

"It was late at night. I wasn't worried about you taking him to the playground or playing an impact sport. While he doesn't fully understand the disorder, he knows that he's not allowed to jump on beds or off furniture."

"Daddy, I'm hungry," Tyler says, emerging from my office with his blue dinosaur. The toy is an absolute favorite, probably because it was from his mother. We decorated the nursery at my house with a dinosaur theme. I had planned on the two of them living with me, I just hadn't expected Wren not to be there.

"Join us for lunch," I say to Elisa, picking Tyler up and carrying him to the elevator. He wraps an arm around my neck, squishing me in the chest with his stuffed friend.

"Are you sure?"

"I wouldn't have asked if I didn't mean it."

# NINE

*Elisa*

WESTON'S GRUMPY voice still plays in my head, yelling at Tyler for jumping off the sofa. Looking at the kid, it's impossible to tell he's struggling with any type of health issue.

I spend a bit of time going down the rabbit hole of googling Vascular Ehlers-Danlos Syndrome. It's genetic. It's almost always fatal. But it doesn't sound like it's too often where it's causing a detrimental effect to a young child.

There are a number of undiagnosed teens who have died from VEDS and I can understand Weston's concern, but I'm also not sure whether this fear is driven by something else. Like whatever happened to his sister.

I want to talk with him about it, but I don't want to push, and it definitely can't be while we're at the office.

Nigel drops off my dress at my place and it's tailored to perfection. The wedding is this Saturday and I'm looking forward to a girls' night with Clare and her friends, celebrating her last night of freedom.

The bachelorette party.

I hang the dress for the wedding in the closet and slip into a dark-green silk dress. It practically looks like a slip but it's sexy as hell. And I want to go out and get noticed.

I shove my phone into my purse and meet up with the girls at the club. I haven't heard from *Steamy Single Dad*. I get the feeling that he's blowing me off. If he doesn't want to meet up with me for coffee, then why text me? Unless he's not the hunk in the photos that he sent.

Guys are notorious for being sleezy, especially on dating apps. Or worse, he's a teen boy, pretending to be a grown man. Eww, who does that and pretends to be a single dad?

I haven't checked the app for any other dates, since *Steamy Single Dad* seems to have bounced out of our chat, leaving me wondering what the hell went wrong.

Is he married?

Engaged?

I head into the club, making sure I'm a few minutes late so that I'm not the first to show up. Clare is already there with a few girls. I'm surprised to see Sloane, I'm guessing that she was invited when we went out a few weeks ago and all met up.

I give Clare a hug and then Sloane, introducing myself to a handful of her friends.

"Are you excited for tomorrow, your wedding night?" Sloane asks, raising her eyes suggestively.

Clare bursts out laughing. "You don't honestly think we've waited." She grabs a shot and tosses it back. The girl already looks hammered.

"Maybe you should slow down," I say. "You don't want to be hungover on your wedding day."

Clare nods. "You're right. We're here to see some strippers!" Clare hollers, and hoots as the guys start coming out on stage.

"This is a strip club?" How did I not notice? I was carded when I came in, but I thought it was because there was alcohol and it was a club.

The men are enticing, easy on the eyes, and damn, do I find it difficult to sit still. There are four of them on stage and my cheeks burn as my eyes roam over their bodies.

"Hottest stripper. Come on, spill." Sloane nudges me, wanting me to partake in their fun.

The guys are all well-built and packing, but I can't say I have the hots for any of them. "Um, maybe the guy in the back."

"He kind of looks like Mr. Grump," Sloane says.

I shake my head. "No way. It's just the dark hair."

Sloane grins, staring at me. "He totally could be Mr. Grump if you had a few more drinks."

There's no way she could know that I slept with Weston Grump. "What are you talking about?" I laugh at her suggestion.

"You have the hots for our boss."

"I do not," I seethe, scowling at her. "He's an annoying bachelor grump. I'll bet he flirts with all the women he meets."

"You would know. You dated him," Clare interjects.

"Why are we all over me about Wes?" I ask.

"Wes?" Sloane catches the nickname before I can pretend it was a slip up. "Wow, next, you'll be calling him baby or Daddy."

"That's insane, and you're drunk." I've seen Sloane trashed and she's not the least bit wasted, but I'm trying to push this conversation away from my hot boss and back to someone else. Anyone else. "Which stripper do you think is hot?" I ask, waiting for any takers. Anyone at all. Clare. Sloane. Or the three other girls, Cali, Ellie, and Tali. Two of them are sisters.

"They're all quite gorgeous, but honestly, I'd rather see my man undressing," Cali says with a snicker.

"She's still in the honeymoon phase," Clare quips.

"Are you recently married?"

Cali shakes her head. "No, but we're recently engaged." She shows me her giant diamond ring. Wow, talk about flashy. I guess he does well, although not a surprise. Clare is marrying a billionaire. Maybe they all run in the same small circle.

"Congratulations."

Clare playfully pushes Cali. "Don't even try to steal my thunder, girl. I'll make you get up there and dance with those strippers."

Everyone bursts out laughing. Clare is all talk and no bite. She used to be a preschool teacher quite some time ago. Now, she spends most of her time as a nanny with Amelia, her soon-to-be stepdaughter.

"I'd like to see that," Ellie says with a wicked grin. "Maybe we can all get on stage and dance with the half-naked men."

"You're all talk." Tali elbows her sister. "I'd totally buy you a dance if you didn't freak out."

"I don't know where to put my hands!" Ellie squeals. Her eyes are wide. She barely looks old enough to be in a strip club and having a cocktail.

"Excuses. Excuses," Tali says.

"Hey! I have a wild idea," Clare quips. "How about we head to the strip club down the street and surprise the boys."

"That sounds like a bad idea," I mutter. "Do you want to see your fiancé staring at other half-naked women?"

"Sure, I'll sit on his lap and give him a dance while he watches another girl on a pole," Clare says cheekily.

We pay our tab and walk the couple of blocks to the club where the boys are. It's chilly outside and my feet are numb from wearing heels in the frigid temperatures, but taking a cab a couple of blocks seems like a waste. And the subway is in the opposite direction.

Shuffling into the strip club, we show our IDs and pay the cover charge to get in. We're escorted to an elevator and upstairs to the main floor. The place is dark, with red velvet chairs, and dimly lit. It takes a few seconds for my eyes to adjust to the lighting.

"There he is!" Clare says, spotting her fiancé in a large corner booth with a bunch of guys. Clare practically dives at him, planting her lips on his. It's a long, tongue-infused kiss and I glance away, not wanting to see the two of them making a kid together.

I glance at the gentleman accompanying him and my brow tightens as I recognize the *Steamy Single Dad* sitting right next to Clare's fiancé.

"Logan!" Cali says, slipping in beside *Steamy Single Dad*, throwing her arms around his neck and planting one on his lips.

"So, that's why you stopped texting," I say.

His brow is furrowed, and I swear he doesn't recognize me. Cali seems like a great girl; I should tell her that the loser has been trying to cheat on her and meet other women. Weren't they engaged?

How long have they been together?

"You're a lying cheat!" I say, pointing at *Steamy Single Dad*.

Footsteps approach from behind. "What's going on?" Weston asks.

Weston is friends with *Steamy Single Dad* and Clare's fiancé?

What are the odds?

"This man, *Steamy Single Dad*, has been flirting with me on the internet, exchanging pictures."

"Whoa! I swear I haven't been on a dating app, ever."

Cali climbs off Logan, clearly confused. "What are you talking about, Elisa?" Cali asks.

I pull out my phone and open the dating app.

Weston swoops right in, grabbing my phone from my hands. "I'm sure it's a mistake."

"What's your problem?" I scowl at him. "Give me back my phone, Wes."

He taps at the screen and accidentally deletes the app. "Oops!"

"Why would you do that?" I smack his arm and yank my phone back. "I'll just download the app again."

"Let me see your phone, Logan." Cali grabs her fiancé's phone and flips through his apps. "He doesn't have any dating apps downloaded."

"See," *Steamy Single Dad* says. "I'm sorry, someone was catfishing you and pretending to be me. But I haven't touched a dating app since forever. I was married when that shit came to fruition and Cali is pretty much the first girl I've met since."

"Who the hell—" I spin around on my heels, staring at Weston. "Tell me it wasn't you."

"You two know each other?" Logan asks, staring at Weston.

"She works for me."

I let out a huff. "That's all it is." I clutch my phone and head for the elevator, pushing the button repeatedly, wanting the elevator cart to appear faster.

"What the hell, man?" Logan says, staring at Wes. "Did you seriously pretend to be me to get a girl?"

"It's not like that."

He doesn't deny it and that's the part that hurts even worse.

I keep pressing the button to go down, but the elevator betrays mc just like everyone else. Finally, the doors ding and Weston hurries after me.

I'm not lucky enough for the doors to shut on him.

"Let me explain," Weston says.

"Explain? Explain how you pretended to be someone else. Hell, not even just anyone, but your friend. Your friend who I might add is engaged!"

I swear everyone is staring at us as the doors finally close and we're alone in the privacy of the world's slowest elevator as it takes its time reaching the main floor.

"I like you and I fucked up, Elisa."

"Which time?" I stare at him. "When we slept together, and you wanted to pretend it never happened. Or maybe it's when we had that shitty date and you kept checking out that blonde chick and staring at your phone. Oh, don't let me forget the newest occurrence of you pretending to be some guy you know."

I'm not even sure how Weston and Logan know one another, and I don't care. The point is that he lied to me.

"I'm not claiming to be a saint. I shouldn't have—"

I cut him off, grateful the elevator opens and I can escape. "I don't care. It doesn't matter. I'm never seeing you again, Wes. It's over."

"We live in the same building," he says as he follows me outside into the frigid winter air. It's icy and feels like snow. The wind whips around, making me clutch my skirt to keep it from flying up. "Let me drive you home."

"You mean, let your driver take me home. You should stay, be with your friends."

Weston exhales a heavy sigh. He grabs his phone, texts Camden, who pulls the car around for me.

"See to it that she makes it home safe," Wes says to his driver.

I climb into the backseat out of the cold. The vehicle has clearly been off, the leather seats chilled, but it's better than outside or dealing another minute with Weston.

I'll head home, write up my letter of resignation, and send it as soon as I'm done.

I'm finished with Wes. Once and for all.

# TEN

*Weston*

RELUCTANTLY, I head back up the elevator to the party. The girls are fun to look at but it doesn't take my mind off Elisa. She's been on my mind since I stepped foot in the club.

What I didn't expect was coming out of the bathroom and seeing her with a group of girls by Levi, the bachelor of the night.

Worse was facing Elisa when she saw Logan. I never thought the two of them would cross paths, which is insane.

I knew Elisa was going to a wedding on Saturday.

So am I, but I didn't think for a second that it was the same wedding. Plenty of people get married on the weekend. Weddings happen year-round, although they are probably more frequent other times of the year.

Maybe I was in denial, thinking I could get Elisa to tell me her deepest, darkest secrets and not have her know that it was me all along.

"You're an asshole," Logan says as I come back upstairs after waiting for Elisa to leave via my driver. He'll be back at the club to pick me up when the night is over.

"So I've been told." I don't let his words soak through me, they roll off. They're meaningless.

"I can't believe I work for you," Sloane says.

"I can't believe you're here," I mutter, and find my empty seat next to Logan.

He's fuming. "I don't get it, man. You have the looks. The charm. The charisma. Girls are always vying for your attention. Why the hell pretend to be me?"

Everyone is staring, watching, and waiting for an explanation. I can't go into detail, not without admitting that Elisa and I slept together.

Sure, the account started out as a little fun, a bad idea that went rogue the minute things got complicated between us. And now I've made them a million times worse.

"I fucked up," I say.

"Damn straight, you screwed up," Logan's fiancé says.

"Cali, settle down."

"No." She moves off his lap, making her point known. "You nearly gave me a heart attack thinking that Logan is cheating on me. I ought to smack you upside the head, but if I leave a mark, tomorrow's wedding pictures will look like shit." This is the first I've met her. He's been going on about her all night, how she likes to rile him up and I can see how that could happen.

The girl is a bit of a firecracker.

"Why are you still here?" Logan stares at me.

"Listen, I said I'm sorry."

"You actually didn't," Cali quips. "You said everything but I'm sorry and I'm guessing that you didn't apologize to the girl you catfished, either."

"Weston, you're welcome to stay and hang out here, enjoy the show," Levi says. It's his bachelor party, I'm here supporting him for his big day tomorrow. "But you're a dumbass if you leave things unsettled with that girl."

"Elisa," Clare says, correcting him.

My answer is silence.

Elisa won't want to see me, and I don't blame her. I betrayed her, burned her, and pretended to be someone I'm not. If it were the other way around, I'm not sure I'd be so forgiving.

I sip my beer, stewing in my seat, refusing to get off my ass.

"I don't know what Elisa sees in you," Sloane says, grabbing a seat next to me.

"Yeah, me either," I mutter. I finish my beer and order another bottle. I don't think I can drink enough to make me forget the damage I've done. I'm lucky Logan didn't throw a punch or threaten to bury me alive.

I don't pay for any private dances. I watch the entertainment, but I never thought I'd go to a strip club and be miserable.

All I can think about is Elisa. How I hurt her. That I shouldn't have lied to her. How, on our date, I distracted the waitress as I was attempting to be polite, and she set Elisa's hair on fire.

It's no wonder Elisa ran out on me during our first and only date. She should have fled. I deserved it.

I finish the second beer, order a third, and Logan comes over, taking Sloane's seat.

"I don't need a lecture," I say before Logan can berate me for what I've done.

"I told you what I thought, that you should be with her tonight instead of us," Logan says. He doesn't hide his thoughts from his friends. He tells it like it is. I'm glad we're still friends even if I did fuck up my life. At least I didn't ruin his.

"She won't want to see me."

Logan shrugs. "You're right. She's going to be pissed. Put yourself in her shoes. You catfished her. That's shitty and I don't care the reasons, whatever you thought would happen, it couldn't. Unless you intended to be a dick to her, but I don't see that in you, Weston. You're normally into banging the next hot girl who walks into a bar, but the whole pretending to be someone you're not, going on dating apps, what is going on? Talk to me."

I exhale a heavy sigh and hang my head.

I'm not proud of my behavior.

"Is this because of Wren?"

"What?" I glance up, not understanding why he's bringing up my sister.

"It can't be easy raising your nephew. Your sister left you with a lot of responsibility."

"He's my son," I say. Legally, I adopted him after Wren's death. He became mine. Biologically, he's my nephew, but I've never thought of him like that for a single day.

"I know you adopted him, his father isn't in the picture. But it's a lot of responsibility, becoming a father overnight. Especially when you weren't planning on it."

"We all knew it was a possibility," I say, glancing up at Logan.

Wren had struggled her entire life with the disorder. When we found out she was pregnant, it had been a tough discussion that we had, if something happened to her during the pregnancy or after, who would take care of her child.

I vowed to be that person.

I was all she had and now I'm all Tyler has.

"Tyler and Wren have nothing to do with Elisa."

"But I think they might," Logan says. "You've kept your heart locked up, afraid to love anyone because you've already lost one person close to you."

"Wren was my sister," I remind him. "It's different."

"Yes, but it's still a great loss and a big change. Tell me I'm wrong."

"You're wrong," I say.

"Then why are you pushing Elisa away? Why lie to her? Why not just tell her you like her?" He tilts his head, staring at me. "Unless you already hooked up with her and she wants more. But then you wouldn't be playing games pretending to be someone else."

I glance away. He's way too close to figuring out what happened.

"You did sleep with her," Logan says, and smirks. He leans back in his chair with a nod. "Was it not good?"

"It was fine." I don't want to have this conversation with him, discussing my sex life.

"Fine doesn't sound hot."

"It was hot, okay." I glare at him. "Sex wasn't the problem."

"What is? Other than you have your head up your ass?"

"I like her, and I don't like anyone. You know I don't do relationships. And even if I wanted to, she's my employee."

"That's an excuse," Logan says, and takes a swig of his beer. "You can find a way around it. You're the owner of the company. Am I right?"

"I don't want other employees thinking that she gets preferential treatment or rumors spreading about her." I'm trying to protect Elisa by keeping a healthy distance.

"Hey, Sloane!" Logan says, and brings her back over toward us to join our conversation.

I groan. Why does Logan have to torment me? "If my buddy Weston here was in a relationship with Elisa, would you be engaging in office gossip about it?"

I glare at Logan. "We're not having sex. Don't listen to him. He's being a jerk."

Sloane stares down at me, unconvinced. "The only jerk I see here tonight is you. And it's obvious that you two shacked up at some point. The sexual tension went from explosive between you to like a bomb went off and you can't look at one another."

"That's not true."

"No," Sloane says, "but you just admitted to it. Mr. Grump, if you're going to sleep with your employees, you have to expect there to be some tension."

"I'm not sleeping with my employees," I growl at her.

"Just one employee," Logan says. "Right?"

I shove my head in my hands. The interrogation is worse than having it out with Elisa. I should have gone back with her, tried to reconcile what I could before it was too late.

"It's fine; you'll see her tomorrow," Levi quips.

"What?" I glance up at him. I was hoping the soonest I'd have to deal with her was Monday morning, at work. Although I've been shuttling her into the office with me, I'm not sure that she'll be keen on taking a ride from me anytime soon.

"At the wedding. She's one of Clare's bridesmaids. The two of you are walking down the aisle together."

"Kill me now," I mutter.

"Does anyone want anything?" Sloane asks, standing up for the bar.

"No, I should call it a night." I've already royally fucked up my life. If I'm lucky, I can try to talk to Elisa tonight, before I have to face her at the wedding.

"You're leaving?" Sloane asks. She glances me up and down, displeased. "Please, tell me you're not going to stop by and visit Elisa?"

I can't make that promise. She lives next door to me, it's not like I even have to go out of the way to see her.

But I have to pick up Tyler first, since he's with Logan's daughter. She's watching the kids for the night.

"We just got here," Levi says. "Sit your stupid ass back down. You'll apologize tomorrow, when you're sober."

"Fuck," I grunt, and throw my ass back down into the chair.

"I'm going to take off," Sloane says, and I ignore her. She gives Clare a hug goodbye and they exchange a few words before Sloane heads for the elevator.

I breathe a sigh of relief. I don't want anything that happens tonight to bite me in the ass at work. It's not bad enough the incident with Elisa, but hanging out with my employees at a strip club doesn't seem wise.

"I'm still pissed at you," Logan says, glaring at me. Cali is curled up on his lap, sipping his beer that she stole, an arm possessively wrapped around his neck.

"Me too," Cali chimes in. "I may have just met Elisa, but she was a sweet girl. Why the hell would you do something like catfish her?"

"I wasn't trying to catfish her," I grumble, and swallow the last of my drink. I stand, needing a refill and not waiting for anyone to come around to the table to serve us.

I don't bother asking the rest of the group if they want anything. I stalk up to the bar and order another beer.

I pay my tab and grab my drink, but I don't take it back to my seat. I don't deserve to sit with those guys after what I've done.

I hang my head, not the least bit enjoying myself. I should go home, pick up Tyler, and call it a night. Tomorrow is going to be a long day.

Clare stalks up to me, glancing me over from head to toe. "I can't decide if you're an asshole or just an idiot."

I glare at her. "I get it, I fucked up. Can we leave it alone?" I'm tired of being reminded that I ruined a perfectly good, well, whatever the hell that we had going for us.

"No, I have half a mind to dump your ass from the wedding party, but you're Levi's groomsman, not mine. You're lucky he's forgiving you, because I don't think you deserve it. Not without a lot of groveling."

"Duly noted," I mutter, sipping my beer.

I pretend not to care what Clare thinks, but she's friends with Elisa. And friends or not, I'm not blind to the mistakes I made.

"Are you going to tell us why you did it?" Clare asks.

I nurse my beer, wanting to end this conversation as quickly as it started. "No."

Clare folds her arms across her chest. "That's not an acceptable answer. And no wonder she calls you Mr. Grump."

I snarl at her. "That's my last name."

"Yeah, well, it's fitting," Clare quips.

I down the last of my beer. "I'm going to call it a night," I say. Clare doesn't stop me. This time Logan lets me go, deciding perhaps I'm not worth the hassle of making me stick around. He's preoccupied with Cali.

I text Camden, informing him that I'm heading down and ready for a lift. By the time I reach the front doors, the vehicle is double parked, with the hazard lights flashing. He ushers me into the backseat, opening the door for me.

"Thanks," I mumble, climbing into the vehicle. The leather is warm. How long had he been sitting in here, waiting for us?

"Are we picking up your son or heading home, sir?" Camden asks.

"We'll pick up Tyler on the way home."

I sit back, staring out the window. It's chilly outside, cold enough to snow. There are a few stray flakes that flutter down but not enough to cause a commotion.

I nearly doze off when the vehicle stops, and Camden slams the front door as he comes around to open the back for me.

"I'll just be a few minutes," I say, forcing back a yawn as I hurry inside the hotel and up to the room.

I should have probably left Tyler at the hotel and let him stay the night for a sleepover. It turns out Levi's mother was on hand to help Julianna with the kids.

But I'll admit I'm a tad overprotective with my son.

After what happened to Wren, I can't help but worry. I never did find out who Tyler's biological father was, my sister refused to tell us when she was pregnant, insisting that it was better for everyone if he wasn't involved.

And there was no after she was pregnant... She died in childbirth.

———

I arrive with Tyler to the Luxenbergs' second home. It seems strange for a billionaire to have a wedding in his backyard. But he has acres of property and trees that go on for miles, offering a picturesque view.

I'd have expected the wedding to be someplace exotic and hard to book. Perhaps a warm destination, like the South Pacific or Caribbean, especially given the fact that it's the middle of winter in New York.

While the venue is one of his many homes, they didn't spare a single expense. There are lights hanging outside, and while it's still daylight I imagine it'll be quite beautiful tonight for pictures, while the festivities continue into the early hours.

Inside the home, there are a number of long wooden tables and matching chairs, a gorgeous setup for dinner.

Outside, there is fresh snow, with evergreens that line the property. There's no one for miles and while the ceremony will be outside, along with pictures, most of the festivities will be held indoors.

I still can't believe Clare wanted to get married outside in the snow and Levi went along with it.

Love.

It makes people do crazy things for each other.

I'm happy for the two of them, and I'll admit the fact it's a nontraditional wedding makes me more excited to be here. I'm thrilled for Levi and Clare, but just the thought of marriage makes my stomach flop. It's final. And what if the person you're marrying turns out to be completely different than the person you lived with and dated?

I've heard horror stories from Levi about Clare's ex-husband. How they had to pay him to go away and leave their family alone.

What kind of a monster chooses money over love? Then again, they were already separated, and he was stalking her. There were probably a number of red flags, but it's not a conversation that I dove into further with Levi. And I barely know Clare.

The first time I met her was when she was with Elisa.

Small world.

Tyler was invited to be a part of the wedding party as the ring bearer. He looks absolutely dashing in his little black tux, his hair recently trimmed and slicked back with a little extra gel to keep it in place.

He's bouncing up and down inside by the back door. It's chilly outside and I've got his winter coat wrapped over his shoulders until it's time for pictures and the ceremony.

"Daddy, can I play in the snow?" Tyler asks.

"Not today, buddy." I sweep him up into my arms and spin him around.

"Put me down!" he squeals with laughter. "I'm a big boy."

"Okay, okay." I can't hide the grin on my face. But it vanishes when I glance up at Elisa. She's wearing a long black dress, but she did well not to outdo the bride.

Nevertheless, she's still stunning and radiant.

The moment her eyes land on me, she glances away and stalks outside, past me without a word. I'm definitely getting the cold shoulder from her, but it could be worse. Elisa could be making a scene and tossing water in my face, or some other beverage, to remind me that she's pissed.

At least she has enough sense not to ruin Levi and Clare's wedding day.

"Daddy, I want to play in the snow," Tyler whines. He wiggles out of his coat, dropping it onto the ground before stalking outside, his little feet sinking into the fresh snow, leaving a trail behind him.

He's not the first to go out into the snow, but my son chose to ignore the shoveled path in favor of thick, fresh snow to pounce. His pants are drenched along with his shoes, and at some point, he's going to grow chilly. I brought an extra change of clothes, but I can't put him in it before the wedding starts.

"Tyler, get your butt back inside," I growl at him.

He stomps through the snow, kicking it in every direction before he sticks his tongue out at me, daring me to chase after him.

The terrible twos don't stop at two. I don't know how I'm going to manage when the kid is a teenager if this is just a taste of the trouble I'll have to put up with.

I'm not the most patient man. I try, but raising a kid wasn't part of my plan.

"No!" Tyler sticks his tongue out at me defiantly and runs in the opposite direction.

Seriously?

He's running toward Elisa. Her back is to him as she stares at the scenery, taking all of it in. She's beautiful, her skin several shades darker than the snow, but she still blends in against the stark contrast of her dark gown.

She's easy on the eyes, but when hasn't she been? Her hair is pinned up for the ceremony and I want to remove the bobby pins and clip and watch her locks cascade down around her shoulders.

There's something incredibly sexy about watching her loosen up, like she's divulging a secret and revealing a piece of herself, meant only for my eyes and ears.

Why is it I can barely stop thinking about her? She invades my dreams at night and my thoughts during the day. She steals my breath, my soul, and my heart with a single longing glance.

Dare I say that I'm falling for her? It was never part of the equation. She was supposed to be my employee, a girl who handles my appointments and fetches coffee for me.

When the hell did all of that change?

Had it been when she watched my son after his nanny had a heart attack?

It could have been the night we were tangled together in the sheets in my bed. I still smell her scent in my room when I'm falling asleep.

I'm sick. It's an addiction I can't untangle from, craving her like I need air to fill my lungs and give me life. She's the cure to my starving soul.

Tyler rams straight into Elisa, like a football player trying to tackle her.

# ELEVEN

*Elisa*

THE AIR IS chilly outside with snow under my shoes. In the distance, I hear Weston shout for his son, but I ignore them, letting his voice drift in the wind.

I'm struck from behind by a small force that topples me forward into the icy cold snow. My hands dart out in front of me to catch myself as I'm pummeled into the white wetness beneath me.

Tyler's giggles erupt from behind as he clutches my legs, keeping me pinned down.

Where the hell did he learn to do that?

Weston grunts and trudges hastily through the snow, grabbing his son off me. "Tyler, that's enough!" he scolds. "What did we talk about? You have to be careful."

I laugh under my breath and Wes offers me a hand to help me stand.

"Thanks," I say, taking his hand while he has Tyler slung around his hip. The kid is soaked from the snow and so am I.

I wipe the remnants of snow from my dress. It was chilly outside but now I'm freezing.

"Come on, let's get you both inside and warmed up," Weston says. His hand falls to my lower back as I head for the clear pathway and hurry to the hearth to get warm.

I wrap my arms around myself; the cabin is plenty warm with the heat cranked and the fire crackling offering extra comfort. I stand in front of the blaze and Tyler joins me. He's shivering from head to toe and Wes emits a heavy sigh.

I suppose now isn't the time to ask if he received my email, the resignation letter that I sent last night.

I don't remember every word that I wrote, hopefully it wasn't embarrassing, because I was slightly more than tipsy from the party. But I'm not the one to be ashamed of my actions.

Weston was the one pretending to be someone else online.

Why would he do that to me?

Did he think he was being funny, trying to catfish me?

Does he think I can't get a date?

"Tyler, what do you say to Elisa?"

"I'm sorry," he says, staring up at me with his vibrant gaze. "Will you forgive me?"

"Maybe you should take one out of his playbook," I say, glancing at Weston. I shuffle my feet, grateful I opted for the black fur-lined boots instead of heels with my dress. At least my toes are warm, that's the only thing on me that's comfortable at the moment.

"I get it, I messed up," Wes says, eyeing his kid.

"You royally messed up," I emphasize. This isn't a little mistake that can be fixed with a bandage and an apology. "What were you thinking?" I hold up my hand, deciding that I don't want to hear his lame excuse.

"I'm sorry," Weston says.

"It's not enough, Wes. What you did, it's unjustifiable. I can't... I can't work with you anymore."

"What?" His brow furrows and his jaw tightens. "What do you mean you can't work with me, Elisa?"

Shit.

Did he not get the email that I sent with my resignation attached? I did send it last night, didn't I?

It had been well after two in the morning when I'd finished writing the letter and hit send.

"My resignation," I say, and clear my throat, trying to find the confidence to tell him he's a dipshit to his face. Except his three-year-old kid is staring up at his father, starry-eyed, like Weston is the ultimate hero.

"You can't resign," Weston says.

"I already emailed you my notice. You didn't get it?"

"I haven't checked my phone. We got up this morning and started getting ready for the wedding. It's been a busy day," he says.

He runs his fingers through his thick dark hair and bites down on his bottom lip, his gaze flinching. "I don't accept your resignation."

"You haven't even seen it."

"Well, pretend I did. I still don't accept," Wes says.

The noise in the room grows louder as it becomes more crowded with guests getting ready for the wedding to begin.

"Are you always this bullheaded?" I ask, stepping closer, coming toe-to-toe with him.

His hot breath hits my cheek, and he leans closer, his gaze on my lips. I swear he's going to kiss me.

I inhale sharply. I'd take a step back but there's nowhere to go. We're trapped between the fireplace and the crowd of attendees gathering inside the giant space before stepping out into the cold to take their seats for the short ceremony.

"Only when it comes to getting exactly what I want," he says.

"Which is what?" I ask, staring up at him.

"You."

I don't believe him.

He doesn't want me. If he did, he wouldn't be playing these games, pretending to be someone else online. What the hell is wrong with him? I'm trapped.

The commotion grows louder and more boisterous as Levi whistles and gets everyone's attention. The crowd settles momentarily while he gives orders for everyone except the wedding party to get their asses outside because the wedding ceremony is about to begin.

The crowd disperses and I flee at the first opportunity before Weston can turn around and realize that I'm gone.

Besides, I'm one of Clare's bridesmaids. It's expected for me to be there and walk down the aisle. I hurry upstairs where the girls are getting ready. Clare is already in her black gown, a huge smile on her face. She's stunning, radiant, and the grin on her face lights up the room.

"Let's do this!" Clare squeals, and we head out with Cali checking to make sure the boys are ready and the guests are seated.

I ignore the chill with the loss of the fireplace and head down the stairs ahead of the bride. I step down, following behind Ellie, when my gaze lands on Weston.

"Go sit down," I scold. "The wedding is about to start."

"I know. I'm walking you down the aisle."

"Fuck," I mutter, unable to contain myself. Weston glares at me, immediately covering Tyler's ears to keep him from overhearing us.

"Daddy," Tyler grumbles, and wiggles out of his hold.

"It's almost time. Two more minutes," he says.

We're all crowded near the door, wanting to watch while also trying to maintain some semblance of order.

Weston takes Tyler's hand and watches from the open door, waiting for the music to begin. The flower girls go first, starting with Amelia, Levi's daughter. She sprinkles black rose petals along the packed snow-covered ground as she gracefully strolls down the aisle.

"You're next. Remember what we talked about?" Weston hands Tyler a small black pillow with a ring tied on by a dark-red ribbon.

I'll admit that I was surprised when I found out her wedding color was black, with a hint of red mixed in every now and then. But she's been married once, and she did the big white wedding with all the proper superstitions, and that didn't turn out.

I'm happy for them but, at the same time, a little bit jealous. Not the envious kind. It's more like I want that for myself.

But now, with my grumpy ex-boss and ex-whatever the hell it is that we shared—one wild night together was clearly a mistake.

Knowing better and doing better aren't mutually exclusive. I knew I shouldn't sleep with him, but I wanted to and damn, was it hot.

And the way he is with his son, it just makes my stomach flutter with butterflies.

I don't want to forgive Weston. What he did to me should be unforgivable. Catfishing me.

Why even do it?

Was it a game to him?

My stomach tosses and turns just thinking about it, the late-night conversations I shared with him, and how I actually thought he was a nice guy.

That's on me.

Tyler pauses down the aisle and turns around, glancing back at his father.

Weston gestures for him to turn around and keep walking.

From the entryway, it's a cute moment, and I feel like I'm eavesdropping on the two of them.

The processional continues with the two of us, and I suck in a breath and my distaste for Weston as he offers me his arm.

I force a smile, but I want to stomp his toe and demand he get his hands off me.

The music continues, and we step outside into the chilly winter air. It's gorgeous and freezing at the same time. I'm trying my best not to shiver, which is an impossible task, even with heat lamps positioned all along the walkway and in the front behind the bride and groom.

Goosebumps cover my arms; the dress I'm wearing is cute but not the least bit warm for outdoor festivities.

Thankfully, the ceremony is quick, and I'm grateful when they exchange vows, rings, a heated kiss, and we're all ushered back inside the warmth of the cabin.

I shuffle my way back inside, doing my best to avoid Weston. Not that it matters. His son seems to recognize me and waves with a wild grin before barreling over toward me through the crowd.

"Tyler!" Weston shouts over the music and loud chatter. It's like he's dodging traffic, trying to navigate his way to me while Tyler has the advantage, sneaking between people's legs and shimmying his way without slowing down for a second.

I bend down, this time aware that he's heading right for me. "Hey, Tyler," I say, and open my arms for him to come barreling into me instead of him knocking me over twice in one day.

At least this time we're both dry from the snow.

He's a fit of giggles, and his eyes are wide as he throws his arms around my neck and plants a kiss on my cheek.

I scoop him up into my arms just as Weston catches up to his son.

"Tyler, you're not supposed to be running off from me," Weston says.

Tyler sticks out his tongue, not caring to listen to his father.

The doors that were open earlier, allowing a cold gust of wind inside, have been shut. "That's not very nice," I say, staring at Tyler. He buries his arms in my chest and rests his head against my shoulder.

"Here, let me take him," Weston says.

Tyler grips tighter to my neck, and I don't think the boy is about to let go anytime soon.

"It's okay, I don't mind," I say, rubbing his back.

Weston is staring at me, and I can't decipher what the hell is running through his mind.

"You're good with him," he says.

Is he really paying me a compliment? After what happened last night, I just want to get away from him. But that seems to be the furthest thing from happening right now.

I exhale a heavy breath. "Thanks."

Weston leans forward, brushing a strand of my hair out of my eyes and behind my ear. "I really am sorry about last night."

Does he not get it? "Are you sorry I found out?" I ask. "Because you've been pretending to be someone else for a lot longer than since last night."

Tyler stirs against me and pulls back. He must sense I'm fuming, and he wiggles out of my arms. I put him down on the floor, and Wes scoops him up before he can tackle anyone else.

"He could be a footballer," I say, offering a wry smile. I'm trying to change the subject, and since I can't seem to escape Weston, I may as well talk about something we both like—his kid.

I'm trying to be civil and polite. I don't want to ruin Clare's wedding day over something that happened between Weston and me.

I should never have let it get that far, sleeping with him—my boss. It was a mistake.

"That's never going to happen," Weston says.

"Oh. Concerned about concussions?" I ask. There's a darkness that clouds his gaze, and he flinches. My stomach flops, remembering the kid's condition. I bite down on my bottom lip to keep from saying something else insensitive.

"I'm concerned about..." He shakes his head. "Never mind, forget it." He carries Tyler away, like I said something to offend him.

I'm the one who should be mad at him for what he did. Catfishing me. Not the other way around!

He stalks across the room toward his buddies, and I'm surprised Logan doesn't appear the least bit mad at him at first glance.

Did he forgive Weston?

"Elisa!" Cali squeals, and throws an arm around me. We met the previous night, but apparently, we're now best friends.

"Hey," I say, and force a smile. "Having fun?" She has a glass of wine in one hand and a little boy on her hip. He has his mother's hair and most definitely his father's eyes.

I didn't realize that she had kids.

Are all of Weston's friends parents?

"Yeah, Clare and Levi have such a lovely home," I say, taking in the atmosphere.

"How are things with you and Weston?" Cali asks, getting right to the point. "I mean, that was a total dick move that he made with the online profile."

I glance from Cali to her son, surprised by her language. "Complicated," I say, as if that sums up everything that's happened.

"You look bored. Come hang out with me and the girls," Cali says, insisting that I follow her. Ellie and Tali are standing next to Logan, speaking with Weston and another girl who's definitely a teenager.

My stomach is back to being all butterflies when I join them, and my gaze lands on Logan. It's weird to have thought that I'd been conversing with him when, in fact, it had been Weston all along.

"Elisa!" Tyler squeals, and throws out his arms to me once again, like I wasn't just holding and cuddling the kid five minutes ago.

"I think you've had enough Elisa time for a while, kiddo," Weston says.

"It's okay," I say, offering to take Tyler for a few more minutes. It's a distraction from last night, from the lies, from everything that makes me uncomfortable. I'd rather hide and not be the least bit social, but that's not why I'm here. It's Clare's wedding day.

And since Weston isn't leaving, I need to find a way to deal with him.

Tyler throws his arms around me again and drops kiss after kiss on my cheek.

"I swear if I didn't know any better, he has a massive crush on Elisa," Cali says.

The room is suddenly warmer. "Like father, like son," I say, and bite my bottom lip.

Tyler gives me a giant hug, and I ruffle his hair, watching him bat his eyes up at me. The kid is absolutely adorable.

"Daddy, I have to potty," Tyler interrupts, and I hand him back to Weston to find the bathroom.

Weston and Tyler hurry through the crowd, and I breathe a sigh of relief.

"It is kind of cute how they both have a crush on you," Cali says.

"Yeah, but Weston isn't actually Tyler's biological father," Logan says to Cali. "I told you that story, didn't I?"

"What?" That catches me off-guard. "He's not?"

"Tyler is his nephew. His sister died in childbirth. I'll let Weston tell you the rest, but he's a tad overprotective given the circumstances surrounding her death."

My stomach drops to the floor. He never said a word about being Tyler's uncle or whatever happened to his sister.

"Overprotective?"

"Not my place to say, but I'm glad you're talking to him," Logan says. "I've known Weston since we served together, and while he's a bit dumb for stringing you along online, he likes you. I think the fact that you both work together just complicates matters."

No kidding. I exhale a breath. "Yeah, that won't matter any longer. I already tendered my resignation," I say.

"You did?" Cali says, her eyes wide. The little boy in her arms curls against her chest, burying into her. "How'd Weston take it?"

"He's in denial," I say.

"Do you have another job lined up?" Cali asks. "That's why you're quitting, right?" She pins me with her stare, and I shift awkwardly on my feet.

I don't want to lie to her. "It's just not a good fit, working for Mr. Grump," I say.

A wry grin spreads across his face. "Mr. Grump. That does describe Weston a little too well."

Cali smacks Logan in the shoulder. "Like you weren't a grump when we first met?"

He laughs and glares at her playfully. "Me? You were the one scaring away all the customers at the shop in my resort with your outburst on how high the prices were."

"I wasn't wrong. I'm never wrong," Cali stares him down.

I shift uncomfortably on my feet. The two of them seem to be emanating steam but not in the angry, I want to storm off kind of way. I swear whatever passion those two evoke caused that little bundle in Cali's arms.

I take a step back, the heat between them is too much for me right now. I head toward the bar, grabbing an Amaretto Stone Sour, wishing I could disappear for the rest of the festivities.

Grabbing my drink, I take a sip and bump into Weston.

"Where's Tyler?" I ask, taking a sip of my drink. I'm surprised Weston isn't chasing him around.

"I dropped him off with Julianna."

"That's Cali's daughter, right?" I ask.

"Logan's daughter, Cali's the step-girlfriend." His brow is furrowed, like he's trying to figure out the relationship. "What are you having?" he asks, nodding toward my drink.

"Amaretto Stone Sour."

"Girly."

"Well, I am a girl." I shift on my feet; his stare is overwhelming. I can't keep doing this with him. "I'm serious about quitting, Wes."

It only lasts a second before Weston's eyes widen.

"What?"

He heard me.

He probably didn't like what he heard, but he caught every word.

I give him silence. Why doesn't he just grab his phone and read my letter of resignation? Is that too much to ask?

"Why?" He tries again, because I don't answer him quick enough.

"We don't work well together."

"That's bullshit, and you know it." His gaze tightens, and he takes a step closer, invading my personal space. His breath is hot. His masculine scent is overwhelming as it tickles my nose. It's a mix of juniper, spice, and evergreen. Like he bathed in the snow-covered forest.

"I know I shouldn't have slept with you." I refuse to lower my stare. "And you shouldn't have catfished me."

He emits a heavy sigh, but he doesn't pull back. "You're right. I was an idiot. I wanted to know what was going through your head after that night together. You've been distant and pulled away from me and since we work together—"

"And you thought pretending to be someone else, a stranger, was going to make us closer?" I want to slap him upside the head. I'd throw my drink in his face if it didn't taste so damn good.

"I'm sorry."

"Apology not accepted."

# TWELVE

*Weston*

SHE CAN'T SERIOUSLY BE QUITTING. All because of me? I realize she's angry with me for catfishing her. That was a dick move, even for me.

But she can't quit.

"I don't accept your resignation."

"It's not up to you. You can't force me to work for you."

"No one's forcing anyone to do anything," I growl at her.

Why the hell does this woman frustrate me so damn much?

She stares at me, sipping her sweet drink, her gaze never wavering. "Good."

"We never should have slept together," I mutter. It doesn't matter how good it was, how right it felt, this disaster of epic proportions is entirely my fault. I should have kept my dick in my pants.

"No shit," she mutters, and takes another sip. I pull the glass from her hands, tossing it back, swallowing every last drop. "What the hell?" She smacks my arm, and her nose twitches. I think she might actually lose it, and I wouldn't blame her.

I deserve her wrath.

I slam the glass down on a nearby table, my arms long enough to reach without having to move the slightest bit away from Elisa. "Get your own drink," she scowls and kicks me in the shin.

Fuck!

I grimace and, without thinking, shove her back up against the wall, pinning her against the wooden slats.

Involuntarily, she shivers. I imagine it's the cold surface and doesn't have anything to do with me pressed up tight against her.

"You're an asshole." She stares up at me.

"I never claimed to be nice or gentle." That isn't me.

"You're certainly not a gentleman," she seethes. If people could spontaneously combust, the amount of heat and anger she's giving off would be enough to physically burn me.

"I never claimed to be," I growl, and capture her lips with mine, ending our argument with a fiery kiss.

She bites my bottom lip, but I don't pull away. My hands wrap snugly around her waist, pulling her tighter and pressing her up against me. I want her to feel what she does to me.

She gasps, and I take it as an opportunity to shove my tongue into her mouth. The anger seeps away slowly at first, like ice being chiseled away. The kiss deepens as she succumbs to her desires.

When she stops fighting me, her fingers grip my arm, digging into my flesh, marking me with her nails. She pulls me tighter, wrapping her arms around me, and I hear the sweet harmony of her moan nestled in the back of her throat.

I should pull back, give us space, or at the very least find a closet for the two of us to sneak off to, but I can't stop kissing her. And she must feel the same way.

Her tongue glides into my mouth, hungrily taking what she wants, only making my desire for her grow. Every taste, touch, and moan makes my cock grow harder. Does she have any idea of the power she holds over me?

I never intend on telling her. It's one secret that will die with me, and hopefully not anytime soon.

Someone clears their throat, and I want to tell them to back the fuck off, but we are at a wedding, and I don't think this is what Levi had intended when he said he wanted his guests to enjoy the reception at his cabin.

"What?" I growl at the offender who is interrupting my good time with Elisa. I reluctantly pull away from the spicy raven-haired girl. Her cheeks are flushed, and her chest rises and falls with soft pants as she tries to catch her breath.

Levi stares back at me, one arm wrapped around his new bride's waist. "I have to admit, if I thought anyone would be shacking up at our wedding, it would be us."

Clare jabs him in the hip with her elbow. "I'm not playing tonsil hockey with you in front of our family and children."

"Children?" Elisa repeats, her eyes blinking slowly.

Levi has one daughter, Amelia.

Clare bites down on her bottom lip and glances away. "There are plenty of children here that don't need to learn about the birds and the bees from us. Or from the two of you."

"Nice save there, *Airplane Girl*."

Clare jabs him a second time in the ribs. "Watch it, *Panty Thief*," she retorts.

"Panty thief?" I lock my gaze on Levi. "This is a story I haven't heard." There has to be some type of explanation for how he earned the nickname. But do I want to know? Tormenting him should be pleasure enough.

"And you're not going to hear it," Levi says, cutting me off. "I'm happy to see the two of you getting along but let's not give the guests an X-rated show."

"We were just kissing," Elisa stammers, as if they didn't just catch the two of us making out.

"Yes, which leads to—" Clare rests a hand on her abdomen.

"Wait? Are you pregnant?" Elisa gasps and brings her hand up to her lips.

"Shh." Clare gestures for her to lower her voice. "We haven't told anyone yet."

"Congratulations times two," I say, wanting to mirror the sentiment, but the thought of having a kid honestly terrifies me. I've got my nephew whom I'm raising, and the thought of two kids, I don't know how Levi and Clare will manage. Although I suppose Amelia is a few years older than Tyler and doesn't have the health issues that he's faced with, either.

Levi pulls Clare against him. "We should make the rounds," he says. "Then get you seated and something to eat."

"I'm pregnant, not fragile," Clare mutters. She gives us both a smile before he ushers her toward other guests.

"Can we talk?" Elisa asks, staring up at me, her eyes bright and wide.

I exhale a sharp breath. "Yeah, that's probably a good idea." As much as I want to go back to what we were doing, it's not going to solve anything.

I don't want her to quit over what happened between us. I'd rather she not quit at all, but I can't force her to work with me, and if we continue to work together, we can't sleep with one another.

Not that there's a lot of that happening.

It was one time.

And so easily, I can recall what it feels like to be buried inside her. My cock twitches with the memory.

It's snowing outside, a light dusting, and frigid. Instead of opting for outside, I lead her up the back stairwell and find a quiet room for the two of us to talk.

Wordlessly, she follows.

I open the door, flip the light switch, and gesture for her to step inside. Her heels clack over the wooden floorboards as she steps into the room. It's clearly Amelia's bedroom, with a princess canopy over the bed and purple sparkly curtains.

Elisa tugs her bottom lip between her teeth and folds her arms across her chest. "That kiss downstairs... we shouldn't, we can't, Weston."

"Why?" I ask, pinning her with my gaze. "You already quit. I'm no longer your boss." If that's the reason, I'm not letting her use it as an excuse. I step closer, invading her personal space.

"It's more than that," Elisa says, staring up at me. "You were a shit to me, Weston."

"And I'm sorry," I say. "I shouldn't have pretended to be someone else online. That was a dick move."

"Yes, it was," Elisa says, and slowly, I see the resolve crumble around her. Like the wall built up around herself is breaking away.

She shuffles her feet and I step closer. "Tell me the real reason you're quitting."

She huffs softly under her breath, her gaze staring down, unwilling to meet my stare. "Elisa?" I want her to answer me.

"Do you honestly expect me to come back into the office?" Her tongue darts out, sticking out to the side as she exhales a heavy sigh. "I'm giving you space. It's what we need. Maybe if we weren't next door neighbors—"

"We won't be for much longer."

"What?" That catches her attention, and she glances up at me.

"It doesn't bother you that we work together, only that we live next door to one another?" I'm a bit perplexed by her logic.

"That isn't it. Didn't you just move into the building?"

"It was a temporary arrangement. My house was getting renovations done, since they found asbestos in the siding and roofing and, in addition, lead paint in the original trim work."

"You mean you don't live in a condo? Of course you don't. You're a billionaire. You could own the entire building." The response she mutters more to herself than to me. I ignore it, well aware of how much I make and my net worth.

"Pretty soon, I should be moving out. The arrangement was never intended to be permanent."

"But you'd still be my boss if I stayed." She chews her bottom lip.

"Yes, that is what I'm suggesting."

She pinches her eyes shut momentarily. "You frustrate me. Do you realize how much you drive me crazy? And what was Logan going on about downstairs with Tyler being your nephew?"

"He told you that?" I can't help but feel anger shoot through me like a bolt of lightning. "He had no right!"

"Don't shoot the messenger," she says, scowling. She's toe-to-toe with me and refusing to back down.

"That wasn't his place to talk about what happened with my sister or Tyler."

Her hand reaches out, brushing gently against my arm. "He didn't tell me anything about your sister. Only that you can be a tad overprotective."

"I don't have another choice," I bite out. "Someone has to look out for Tyler. He's too young to understand his condition. I never told you about Wren being his mother because I didn't want you to look at me or like Tyler the way you're staring at me right now."

"How am I staring at you?" Elisa asks, her voice soft. "With concern?" She interlaces our hands together, giving my palm a firm squeeze. "I know you care about Tyler."

"Damn right, I'd give my life for his. I'd trade away his condition if I could, and I swear, I've tried. You'd think being a billionaire would help. I run fundraisers, I donate to medical research and have an entire suite dedicated to researching his condition, but it isn't enough."

"It will probably never feel like enough," Elisa says.

I lean in, capturing her lips unabashedly. Taking what I crave, what I need, like air to survive. She doesn't stop me. Elisa doesn't so much as pull away. Instead, I'm met with eagerness and warmth as her fingers fist the lapels of my suitcoat.

"Please don't quit." I don't want to beg or plead for her to stay. But if she's leaving because of me, abandoning her job because I'm the asshole, that isn't fair to her.

"I can't be making out with my boss," she whispers, staring up at me. Her intense gaze makes my insides burn wanting another taste, craving to steal her breath away.

"Does that mean you're not leaving me?" I growl. The question comes out possessive, gruff, and like she belongs to me.

Her tongue darts out, and her gaze tightens. "I will stay on one condition," she says, and I swear she's on her tiptoes, teasing me with those ruby lips. Her breath mingles with mine.

I want to lean in again and kiss her, taste her, press her against the wall and fuck her.

I refrain from answering with *anything*, because that's how I feel right now, I don't want her to walk away from the job or, more importantly, from me.

"Dance with me," she says, and a wry grin spreads across her face.

"That's it?"

She smirks and grabs my arm, her hand sliding down until she reaches my fingers, intertwining our digits as she pulls me downstairs toward the dance floor through the crowd of guests.

The music slows as we approach the dance floor, and the smile vanishes from her lips. Like she was comfortable with a fast-paced, trying to embarrass me dancing out on the floor. "Where are you going?" I ask, pinning her with my stare, gripping her hand to keep her from sneaking away.

"The beat... I can't dance to this," Elisa stammers, and I pull her close against me.

"You don't know how to dance with a partner?" I rest one hand at her lower back and the other stays clutched to her hand.

"I didn't say that," she answers, staring up at me. Her eyes sparkle like diamonds, and my breath catches in my throat at how easily I could get lost in her gaze.

"Elisa, is that you?" a gentleman interrupts us.

Her eyes widen and she spins around to face him. The dance floor is crowded, and she brushes up against me. Instinctively, I wrap an arm around her waist.

I can't see the look on her face with her back to me, but he's got a wide grin and he's definitely checking her out.

I don't like him already, and I haven't the slightest notion of how they know one another, but I'd guess it's intimate. At least he wants it to be, based on the way his gaze is fascinated with her body. She doesn't emit the same vibe that he does.

The man isn't the least bit attractive, but that doesn't take away from the fact that he's donning a Rolex and is clearly well-off. Makes two of us. Money isn't an issue for me, but I don't flaunt my earnings. I live comfortably and modestly, some might even say, considering my net worth, but I have all that I need and want.

Well, I did until I met Elisa.

And with the way Beady Eyes is ogling her, it makes my stomach flop. I pull her against me possessively, laying claim to her as if I have the right. Which I don't.

She glances back at me with a raised eyebrow, clearly wondering what the fuck is going on, and I'm silent, my fingers skimming over her stomach, the black material thin as I caress her through the fabric.

Elisa leans back into me harder, like she wants my protection. At least, I hope that's what she's insinuating, because I go with it.

"We haven't met," I say, and with one hand draped around her, the other comes up to introduce myself to the man.

"I'm Connor, Levi's brother," he says.

There's almost no resemblance between Levi and Connor. As if Levi had all the good genes and Connor was dealt a bad hand. I can't imagine Elisa is interested in him. Although that sounds rude. I'm sure on the inside, he's a great guy.

"Weston," I say, introducing myself. "Levi and I are old military friends."

"Ahh," he says with a grin, "one of his bareback buddies."

"Excuse me? What the fuck are you insinuating?" I growl. Even if Levi or I were gay, that's one hell of a shitty way to make an introduction. I step closer, towering over him. My jaw tightens, and Elisa moves aside to keep from getting sandwiched between us as I stare the asshole down.

"It's a joke. Lighten up," Connor says, and runs a hand through his thinning hair.

I refrain from slugging him, if only because this is Levi's wedding, and I don't want to ruin his and Clare's special day.

I ignore Connor and glare at Elisa. "Please tell me the two of you aren't acquainted." I'll vomit if I find out that they slept together or dated.

I'm not typically the jealous type, probably because I don't have time for relationships. My son is the center of my world, and when I'm not taking care of him, I have a business to run.

"We're mere acquaintances," Elisa says, perhaps witnessing the steam that's emanating off me. "If you'll excuse us," she says with a polite smile as she clutches my hand and drags me away from Connor.

"What the hell was that?" I ask when we leave him standing on the dance floor.

"It was about to be his funeral," she mutters, and grimaces when she sees Tyler running toward us. A teenage girl is chasing after him, maneuvering through the guests. Julianna Henderson, Logan's daughter.

"Sorry," Julianna says apologetically.

"Daddy, can we play in the snow?" He points outside as the day has turned to night and a fresh blanket of snow is beginning to fall around the cabin.

I refrain from grumbling, trying to lighten my mood after the run-in with Connor, but I can't quite shake the anger that ruminates through my veins. "No," I say a little too gruffly.

"Please?" Tyler whines, and his bottom lip pouts up at me. The kid has a knack for getting what he wants.

Elisa drops to her knees, meeting my son at eye-level. "How about we find the dessert table and steal a cupcake?"

I open my mouth to object, and she raises an eyebrow, silently warning me to zip it. I gesture for her to go and exhale a heavy sigh.

"I'm sorry, Mr. Grump," Julianna says. "I tried to keep him entertained with Amelia."

"It's quite all right," I say. "I appreciate your helping look after him."

Julianna exhales a breath, like the weight of the world has been lifted off her shoulders.

"Go have fun. Enjoy the wedding," I say, gesturing for her to get on the dance floor.

Julianna gives a bright smile and saunters off.

Am I really that much of a grump that she was worried I'd be upset about Tyler? I grumble under my breath and catch sight of Tyler wearing light pink frosting all over his lips and cheeks. He's a mess.

Elisa has a dab on the corner of her lips from the cupcake she swiped. "Was dessert good?" I ask and lean in, stealing a kiss, tasting the smear of frosting.

"Very," she whispers huskily as I pull back.

"Daddy, carry me." Tyler holds his arms up into the air, getting between Elisa and me.

He doesn't seem the least bit fazed that I just kissed Elisa. Maybe it's no big deal to him? I haven't dated any girls in front of him. It's always just been the two of us. I've been careful to shield him from my dating life.

"You're supposed to be my wingman, buddy," I tease.

"Wingman?" Tyler asks, frowning. Obviously, he doesn't get my reference. I'm waiting for him to throw his arms out like a bird or an airplane.

"It's okay." I kiss his nose, avoiding the sticky mess on his face. "How about we find a bathroom and get you cleaned up?"

Tyler's tongue darts out, trying to swipe away the frosting, but it'll take more than that to conquer the mess he's made. I'm lucky it's not all over his outfit and mine.

"I'll be here," Elisa says, offering a smile, and I exhale a breath. Connor is watching us, standing a few feet away, a near-empty drink in hand.

He keeps checking out Elisa, and I get the sneaking suspicion that the minute I leave her alone, he'll pounce on her like the animal he is.

"No," I say, pinning her with my stare. "Join me upstairs."

She sucks in an anxious breath and glances down at Tyler. Elisa forces a smile. "Sure, whatever you say, boss."

We head upstairs, away from the crowd, and to one of the spare bathrooms to clean Tyler up.

I bring him into the bathroom, flip on the light, and prop him up on the sink.

"Do you need me to stand guard or something?" Elisa asks from the doorframe. "I'm not sure how I can help."

"Connor was checking you out," I say, glancing at her while grabbing a washcloth and dousing it under the sink with warm water. I carefully wash

Tyler's face and hands, making sure not to soak the adorable outfit he's wearing for the wedding.

She folds her arms across her chest. "Jealous?"

I scoff at her suggestion. "No. I was trying to be a gentleman and keep that pathetic ass away from you."

"Daddy said a bad word," Tyler gasps.

"I'll put a quarter in the swear jar when we get home," I mutter.

Elisa grins widely, the smile completely natural and carefree, and she tilts her chin up at me. "I'll bet that sucker is filled to the brim with quarters."

"No," I counter, pinning her with my stare. "I usually just toss a dollar in and figure it'll cover me for the rest of the day."

"No judgment from me," she says, holding her hands up. "I'd probably owe twenty dollars with my sailor's mouth."

I've never heard her swear.

I help Tyler down from the bathroom sink and toss the washcloth in the nearby hamper.

"Daddy, can I have a brother?" Tyler asks.

His question stumps me, especially with Elisa's heated gaze devouring me.

"A what?" Where the hell did that idea pop into his head from?

"I want a baby brother. Like Miles. Can we take him home?"

Miles is Logan and Cali's son. They must have been playing together downstairs. Elisa is grinning, and she covers her lips to keep from laughing out loud. She glances away, and I imagine she's biting on her lip. Does she ever think about me like that? The three of us as a family?

Although I never planned on having kids. I didn't want to be a father, let alone a single dad. It just kind of happened.

"No, we can't take Miles home. He belongs with Cali and Logan," I explain, hoping to avoid any further discussion on where babies come from. He knows it's not a stork, and the kids' picture book that explained the basics about mommies and daddies probably didn't help with any lack of confusion. Given the fact his mother is my sister.

That is one talk we'll have in more detail when he's older. That I'm technically his uncle. One day. I keep pushing it further away.

"But I want a brother," Tyler whines, his bottom lip pouting as he stares up with wide eyes.

Having more kids is out of the question. I had a vasectomy years ago. And I have no plans to reverse it.

That's not to say that I don't love Tyler, because I do, but one kid is enough for me. I can't imagine juggling two kids, especially given Tyler's condition.

"How about we go back downstairs to the party, and you play with Miles?" Elisa says, ruffling Tyler's hair.

He stares up at Elisa with a toothy grin, eyes sparkling like the kid would do anything she asks of him.

"Okay," he chimes with reddish cheeks and dimples that are absolutely adorable. He looks remarkably like a young Wren with the dimples and grin from our childhood photographs.

He clutches Elisa's hand. "I'll take him back downstairs," Elisa says, glancing over her shoulder at me. "Stay here?"

I raise a curious eyebrow, wondering why.

"I'll be right back, then we can talk."

My stomach flops at those words. We're still trying to figure out what the hell we are—hating one another and her threatening to quit one minute, and I'm kissing her the next. She's right, we do need to talk, but I can't help but worry she's going to let me down gently.

"Be quick," I say with a confident smirk, not wanting her to see the pain tearing me apart inside.

## THIRTEEN

*Elisa*

TYLER BOUNCES DOWN THE STAIRS, and we wander through the crowd until I find the playroom. There are toys stacked along the neatly organized shelves and a built-in bookcase with hundreds of children's books.

In the corner is a tent, and massive giggles are coming from inside. Even with the onslaught of music and guests' chatter from down the hallway, I can hear the chatter of children hiding inside.

Tyler drops my hand and charges for the tent, sneaking inside and disappearing with the kids.

After a minute and him seeming fine, I return back upstairs to sit and have a chat with Weston. I don't know what the hell I'm going to do.

Even if I agree to return to work for him, we can't—the two of us have to remain professional. I'm at odds internally with what I want versus what is right.

And does he even want me?

Obviously, that kiss was to keep me from being angry at him, and it mostly worked. I forgive him for being a complete and utter grumphole, but if we work together, then we can't cross that professional boundary, and truth be told, I want him to crawl into my bed.

Talk about complicated.

I take my time returning upstairs. Weston isn't in the bathroom, he's standing in the hallway, his back to the wall, his eyes raking over my body as I stalk up the staircase.

"About damn time." His eyes are practically undressing me.

I'm glad Clare didn't make us wear hideous dresses to make herself look good. She'd never need to do that; she makes a gorgeous bride, and she's an even better friend.

"I managed to secure us a room," Weston says, and takes my hand, leading me down the hallway. He opens the bedroom door, and I saunter inside first.

I step into the room first and turn around, leaving plenty of space between us. I didn't suggest we talk as a euphemism for sex. We need to figure this out if we're going to work together.

He shuts the door behind us, and the music and chaos from downstairs seem to dissipate with the stillness of the room. It's a guest room, unoccupied by the looks of it. The queen mattress is untouched, the bed made. There's no sign of anyone sleeping in here. No luggage. No phone charger on the bedside table. It's clean and empty.

Weston steps closer, stalking toward me, and I suck in a breath. My stomach is doing somersaults. I hold up a hand, having him keep a distance between us. "We're in here to talk," I say. His eyes are filled with hunger.

Is it because of what we did downstairs that has him fueled inside? My body still tingles with the memory of his lips on mine, his hands firm on my skin, possessive.

"Right," he says, and lets out a low breath. "I don't want you to quit. You're too valuable for me to let you walk away." The words spill out before I have time to speak.

That's it. That's the reason he wants me to stay in the position under him? Because he needs me for the job.

I'm not sure why I thought there'd be another reason.

"I won't quit," I say, meeting his intense gaze. "It's not like I have anything else lined up." I offer a faint smile, my lips curving upwards to reassure him that I don't plan on going anywhere.

He gives a firm nod. "Good, I'd hate to think anyone else might get you to themselves."

I get the sneaking suspicion he's not talking about work. "Weston," I say, and exhale a heavy breath. My hands tremble, and I hope beyond measure that he doesn't notice. "If we're working together, I can't... we have to keep it professional."

"Have I ever been unprofessional at the office?" he asks, his eyes boring into mine.

My tongue darts out, trying to think of a time when he was less than professional. "No," I say. "But we can't."

He steps closer, invading my personal space. His scent is woodsy and thick, intoxicating. I should move back, keep a safe distance to remain level-headed, but I don't want to slip out of his grasp.

His hand comes up, his thumb strokes my cheek. A very unprofessional gesture from my boss. "I don't want to keep things business between us. I want you. And I want you to work for me."

I inhale sharply. "Weston," I whisper, staring into his heated dark gaze. He sucks me in and makes my body warm and tingly in the most intimate of places. "What you're asking—"

"Is for us to find a way to make both work."

"It can't," I say, regretfully voicing the words that I don't want to be true. "You have a son, you need to think of him. And a business. I'll always come in third and when staff finds out—"

"They won't find out," Weston insists.

I laugh under my breath. "Seriously? You just made out with me downstairs at Clare's wedding. People talk. The two of us just being friends, it's all I can offer."

He wraps an arm around my waist, pulling me closer. Tighter. I feel his erection pressing into me. "It's not good enough. I want you, Elisa, all to myself. For work, for pleasure, all of it."

His fingers tangle in my hair, undoing the clip holding my locks up, and he grabs a fistful, keeping my head tilted up at him. I don't think he intends to undo the clip, but maybe he does? I've never seen such a brash and bold side of my grumpy boss before and dare I say, I might easily fall in love with him.

"You're mine," he growls. His lips land hard on mine, claiming me, marking me, bruising me with a kiss so intense, even if I wanted to pull away, I couldn't. I don't want to move anywhere but closer to him.

The heat of the room intensifies, the temperature escalates, and the fiery kiss leaves my lips aching along with my other parts, longing for more.

"And what about your other employees?" I whisper as he breaks apart the kiss.

"I don't want to sleep with them," Weston whispers, and his lips trail roughly down my neck. Nipping. Biting. Licking my skin.

I shudder involuntarily and glance down to see the smile growing on his face.

With one hand, his fingers guide up my thigh, seeking his intended destination. "You're wet for me," he whispers into my ear.

My eyes slam shut, not wanting to admit how turned on he's made me tonight. I feel ashamed that I want to fuck my boss. I don't just want to crawl under the covers and make love to him. I want him to claim me, dominate me, and show me that I'm his and his alone.

"Look at me," he commands.

My eyelids flutter open, staring up into his heated dark stare as he swipes his fingers over my wet panties. He pushes the thin fabric to the side, and I gasp in anticipation.

But he doesn't touch me.

"Beg me," he orders, and kisses my lips hungrily, rough and demanding.

"Never," I rasp, but I'm already close to my breaking point. He walks me backward toward the mattress. The backs of my knees hit the soft material.

"Beg me, Elisa."

"I don't beg," I whisper, challenging him. Just because he's my boss, that doesn't mean we're not equals in the bedroom.

Weston takes a step back and loosens his tie.

I inhale sharply, sitting at the edge of the bed, waiting to see what happens next. Is he going to walk away and leave me aching for release because I didn't follow his orders?

My insides ache with need. I'm craving his touch and he's slowly unbuttoning his shirt, watching me as I devour him with my eyes.

"You're turned on," he says with pride. Like he knows which buttons of mine to push.

"Am n-not," I stammer, and he chuckles.

"I like that I make you wet. Don't be ashamed of it," he growls. He tosses his dress shirt onto the floor, not caring that it'll get wrinkled.

I glance at the bedroom door. "Did we lock it?" I ask.

Weston smirks. "Nope." There's amusement in his tone.

"Someone could walk in," I gasp, and move to climb off the mattress, but he blocks me.

"Let them. Unless you don't want this?"

He's giving me an out, a chance to say no, to keep things professional. But it's not what I want.

I want him.

My silence, he takes as acceptance and guides me back farther onto the mattress, straddling me. He grabs a condom from his wallet and removes his trousers while I work the zipper on my dress.

"Leave it," he commands.

He lifts the hem of my dress, pushes my panties aside, and his fingers dance over my slit, discovering my wetness. It coats his fingers, and he plunges two thick fingers inside to ensure that I'm ready for him.

He teases me, his lips covering mine as his fingers fuck me and I clench onto him. I want more. He's rough, but it's exactly what I need and crave in this moment. He tugs my panties down in one swift movement and opens the condom, putting it on before repositioning himself at my entrance.

He pauses, staring down at me. "Are you sure?" he asks for my consent, and I nod in acceptance.

"I need to hear it." He stares down at me. My fingers move over his abs, inching down his body. If he doesn't do it soon, I'll roll us around, take command and fuck him myself.

"I want you," I say, staring up at him, "to fuck me."

My words set off an instinctual fire between us. He growls and buries himself inside me all at once. It's intense and rough, and my fingernails dig into his forearms as he stretches me to accommodate his size.

He bites down on my lower lip, his kisses rough and exploratory as he pushes his tongue into my mouth while his cock drives into me.

It's heaven and sinful all at the same time. I wrap my legs around him, dragging him closer, tighter, deeper. I want to feel him buried inside me as he comes.

He grabs my arms, pinning my hands against the mattress, our fingers tangling together as he fucks me.

My eyes slam shut, the first warmth of euphoria spreading through me like wildfire.

"Look at me," he commands.

My eyelids are heavy, and my breath is raspy as my lips part and I slowly open my heavy lids to stare up at him. I bite my bottom lip as the first wave comes and he crushes my mouth, nipping and biting, riding the wave with me. His pace never slows, it's even and steady until the final crescendo when he moves harder and faster.

"Fuck," he growls, panting hard, gasping for breath when I clutch him like a vise and my insides tremble.

I can't keep my eyes open any longer. It's too intense, too overpowering as my toes curl and warmth spreads through every inch of me.

"Come for me," he rasps into my ear, and his breath sends another tantalizing shudder rippling through my body.

I tremble and clench on as though my life depends on it for survival.

Weston is right there, claiming me, capturing me, and crushing his lips on mine as he rides the euphoric wave with me. Both of us reach our peak together.

He collapses on the mattress and pulls out, stumbling toward the attached bathroom.

I smooth down my dress in case anyone walks in, but moving from the mattress isn't something I feel capable of doing just yet.

I'm exhausted, coated in a sheen of sweat, and my heart continues to gallop in my chest.

Eventually, I sit up after I catch my breath. Weston is cleaning up and putting his suit back on, trying his best to look like we didn't just fuck upstairs at Clare's wedding reception in their house.

She'd have a fit if she knew what we were up to.

Weston retrieves my panties from the floor and slowly slides them up my legs. Even the gesture is sexy, him helping redress me.

"Let me fix your zipper," he says.

I had started to undo my gown when on the mattress. He offers me a hand to stand and gestures for me to turn around. He carefully raises the zipper, ensuring that I'm presentable before returning back to the party.

"Thanks," I say. My cheeks must be burning as I gaze over his body. He's back in his suit, looking sharp and handsome, with no evidence of what we just did. How the hell does he look so calm and collected?

I feel ruffled and unraveled.

His thumb grazes my bottom lip. "Your lipstick is a bit smeared," he says, fixing the mess.

"So is my hair," I say, pointing at the mess. While my hair isn't nearly as long as it used to be when it was blonde, it's still long enough to have in an updo for the wedding. Now it's down and someone is bound to notice.

"Just tell them you let your hair down for dancing," Weston says.

"That's not a thing," I counter.

"Well, it should be. Like girls taking off their heels." He takes my hand, our fingers tangling together. "We'll make this work, you and me."

I still don't know how. "I'm not good at keeping secrets," I say, staring up at him.

"Then we don't keep it just between us."

I smile faintly. "Sloane saw us downstairs."

"So what if she did?" Weston shrugs.

"We work together. Sloane could tell HR or anyone else we work with about us."

His arms wrap around my waist. "Remember, I own the company." His breath mingles with mine, teasing me for another kiss. But his lips don't graze mine just yet. "If you're that worried, we'll go straight to HR. We're not a public entity. There are no board members or trustees whom I report to," he says.

"You can fix everything just like that?" I ask, snapping my fingers. Like he can make everything fine, and I'm the one overreacting.

"Well, there is Marjorie in HR. She'll probably make us both sign something that stipulates it's consensual and that I'm not taking advantage of you."

"And that I won't sue you when things end sourly," I add, already knowing it's more for his protection than my own.

His fingers tangle with mine. "Who said anything about it ending?"

"How many relationships have you had that didn't end?"

He pulls me against him, crushing me with his chest in a tight embrace. "No one has ever made me the feel the way that you do."

I chuckle and wrap my arms around his waist. "And how's that?" I ask, glancing up at him. "Frustrated? Annoyed? Irritated?"

"In love."

His words catch me by surprise. I loosen my grip, prepared to take a step back, but he doesn't loosen his hold. "You can't mean it," I whisper.

We're always butting heads, and this relationship is new and fresh. With Weston, I feel magnetically drawn toward him, but I'm not sure I'm ready to describe that feeling as love. The only time I'd been in love or thought I had, I'd been mistaken. The man had lied to me, betrayed me, and forgotten to mention that he was married.

He guides my chin up, forcing me to meet his stern gaze.

"If I have to prove to you every day that I love you, I will," Weston says.

My breath catches in my throat. "Y-you shouldn't have to do that," I stammer. His words catch me off-guard. "And I really like you too, a lot."

His lips brush against mine. "I should hope so, after what we just did on that mattress." I quickly reclip my hair up, but it likely doesn't look the same as earlier.

He pulls me with him to follow downstairs, and I worry that all eyes will be on me. But no one seems to notice or care that we were upstairs.

I stalk past one of the windows and gasp. Snow blankets the recent path where Clare and Levi exchanged their vows. What had been a few flurries is quickly turning into a snowstorm.

A few guests have already left, and the room is far less crowded, but not everyone has ventured home. Levi stalks toward us the minute he lays eyes on us.

Does he know what we were just doing upstairs?

"The roads will be impassible soon. You both should stay here tonight. We'll find space for everyone."

"That isn't necessary," I say.

"It is," both Levi and Weston say in unison.

Clare saunters over, wrapping an arm around Levi's waist.

"I was just telling them they should stay the night," Levi says.

"We have enough space, but we might need some people to bunk up," Clare says. She's trying to hide the huge grin on her face like she thinks she's playing matchmaker and setting the two of us up to share a room. Little does she know we've already christened the bedroom upstairs.

"I'm sure we can handle sharing a bed." Weston wraps an arm around my shoulders.

"Would Tyler be okay on an air mattress?" Clare asks. "We can put one out for him in your bedroom."

"Yeah, that would be great," Weston says. "Thank you."

"One of the hazards of snow this time of year," Levi says. "If you need to borrow something to wear, Clare can lend Elisa some clothes, and I'm sure I've got something that will fit you, Weston."

"Thanks," we both say in unison.

While I wouldn't ordinarily be concerned about what I'm wearing to bed, the fact is Tyler will be sharing a room with us and I'm not wearing the fancy dress to bed.

The remainder of the evening is spent dancing, drinking, and enjoying the wedding. Clare and Levi are all over each other on the dance floor. It's cute and sickeningly sweet at the same time. Amelia keeps popping up every so often with Tyler in tow.

"I think he's got a crush on her," Weston says, nodding toward Tyler and Amelia on the dance floor. His arms are wrapped around her waist as he stares up at her, grinning brightly.

"What is she, twice his age?" I joke with a slight laugh.

"Dance with me." Weston pulls me onto the dance floor before I can react.

"Any excuse to feel me up in public?" I tease as his hand wanders over my backside.

"I didn't think you'd notice," Weston says with a wicked grin, his eyes shining down at me as he pulls me tight against him.

We sway to the slow rhythm, and the moment stretches on between us. His hands wrapped around me feel natural, and I don't want it to end. Not tonight. Not ever.

His surname may be Grump, but the more I've come to know Weston, the more I see he is kind, caring and would give the world for Tyler. I never thought I'd date a single father, let alone my boss.

The lights in the cabin flicker twice before going out from the snow. There's a rumbling of discontent and concern as the backup generator kicks in to allow the lights and main system to be back up and running. The music is off, though, until the electricity kicks back in.

"Daddy." Tyler scampers over to us, and Weston untangles from my embrace, lifting his son into his arms.

"I think it's about bedtime," Weston says, deciding to call it a night. I glance at my watch. It's nearing midnight, and with one glance outside, I see that the snow is thick and unapologetic. It won't be stopping anytime soon.

Hopefully, we'll be able to shovel out tomorrow and drive back to the city.

Weston helps Tyler get ready for bed, inflating the air mattress with an electric pump and getting him settled.

I give the two of them some space while Clare loans me a pair of pajamas to change into for bed.

Once Tyler is curled up and asleep, I sneak into the darkened bedroom, wearing flannel pajamas and climb under the covers with Weston. It's not sexy but it's certainly warm and cozy.

His arms instantly wrap around my waist, tugging me closer.

I bite down on my lower lip to refrain from giggling and waking the little one sleeping near the foot of the bed.

Weston's lips graze mine, his hands slipping beneath the fabric, palming my breast with one hand and grazing my hip with the other.

Instinctively, my lips part, granting him entrance as he deepens the kiss, rolling me onto my back as he straddles my hips.

"Your son—" I whisper, worried he might overhear us.

"He's a heavy sleeper," Weston says.

I shake my head. "We can't... not with him in the room."

"I wasn't suggesting we have sex tonight," he whispers into my ear. "I just want to touch you." His fingers trail over my bare skin, teasing my stomach and the waistband on my pajama bottoms before gliding his palm up over my breast and teasing a nipple.

My fingers rake through his hair, bringing his lips to mine for another searing kiss. "You're touching is going to lead to other things," I rasp, letting my eyes fall shut. I'm tired, but he's making me feel more alive than ever.

He drops one final kiss on my lips before climbing off me and rolling onto his side. He drapes an arm across my waist before whispering, "Goodnight."

# FOURTEEN

*Weston*

IT'S BEEN six weeks since Levi's wedding. Elisa doesn't spend every night at my place; she's over a few times a week, and I know that will be less frequent with me moving back to the house.

The movers have packed up the condo, and it'll be vacant until the lease is up. No sense in living in the building anymore when I can return home.

Except for the obvious fact that I'll miss my next-door neighbor.

"You're actually leaving," Elisa says, standing in the hallway outside as I carry our luggage out of the condo, heading for the elevator.

"Can you watch Tyler for me while I pack this stuff into the car?" I ask, glancing at her over my shoulder as I hit the button for the elevator.

While the movers have all the boxes and big-ticket items, there are plenty of toys, clothes, and whatnot that need to be brought home. Tyler would miss his stuffed dinosaur among his other favorite toys if I waited for the movers to handle everything. And while they're efficient, they're not me.

I'm a bit of a perfectionist and a control freak. It's something I'm working on at the moment.

"Never thought I'd see a billionaire carrying his own luggage," Elisa says with a smirk. She closes her front door and saunters into my place to watch Tyler.

"Camden called off today. He's got the flu." The elevator doors open, and I shuffle inside with two giant suitcases, a backpack, and a laptop bag. "Thank you."

"Don't mention it."

I hurry down into the bone-chilling winter air and load up the trunk as quickly as possible. The hazard lights are flashing while I'm double parked.

I hurry back upstairs and inside, to see Elisa sitting with Tyler on the sofa, reading a book together.

She pauses when she sees me grab the last set of luggage to take downstairs. "I'm going to miss having you as my neighbor."

I smile and lug the duffel over my shoulder. "It's not like we won't see each other at work every day—" I let the words hang in the air. It will be harder to have late-night rendezvous without Tyler noticing.

Although Elisa does tend to spend a few nights a week waking up in the morning with me. That's been a newer occurrence lately. I don't like when she disappears during the night or early morning without waking me up first.

When did I become so weak that I hate the thought of her not being around? I've never depended on anyone but myself. But I don't have to feel that way around Elisa. She's been a lifeline, helping with Tyler, being supportive, and so much more.

I've contemplated asking her to move in with me, but that's a huge step and I'm not sure it's something she's ready for, a full-time position as Tyler's stepmom. Not that I'm asking her to marry me, but if she moves in, that's where it's heading, at least in my mind.

I finish loading the car with the last of the luggage before coming back to grab my son. His car seat is already in the backseat. I'll just have to buckle him in before heading to the house.

Elisa finishes the last of the book. She chews profusely on her bottom lip, like she has something to say but is holding back.

Tyler climbs onto his knees, wrapping his arms around her neck, clinging to her. The kid loves her.

He's not the only one.

That thought hits me with brevity, and I inhale sharply.

"Is everything okay?" Elisa asks, glancing at me over her shoulder. She moves to stand, but Tyler hasn't let his hold loosen, and she hugs him, holding him to her as she walks across the room toward me.

I avoid answering the question. "You should come by my place tonight, help me unpack."

"Is that the only reason you want me over?" she asks with a growing smile on her face.

"Not the only reason," I say, leaning in and dropping a kiss on her lips.

Tyler monkeys from around her neck to mine, clutching on to me. "Gross," he says, scrunching his nose as we kiss.

"Do you have the address?" I've already put it into her phone for her, but I want to make sure she knows how to get to my place.

"Of course, don't you know, I've been stalking you?" Elisa jokes. Her smile brightens up the room and I can't stop myself from planting another kiss to her lips.

"Stalk me all you want."

There's a prominent knock on the door. It's Theo, one of my personal assistants. He's been helping with the move, handling the logistics, initiating contact with the movers, and is hanging around to facilitate everything.

"Come on in, Theo," I say, gesturing him inside. While everything is already packed, someone has to make sure all the boxes and furniture are loaded onto the truck and brought over to my house this afternoon. That's his responsibility.

"Theo, this is Elisa," I say, introducing them. Theo's a few inches taller than I am. In another life, he could have been a football player. He certainly has the build and stamina for it.

"Nice to meet you," Elisa says. "I could have helped with the movers."

"You do enough work for me. I'm not about to take advantage of you because you're next door."

"That wasn't what I meant," she whispers, pinning me with her stare.

Theo clears his throat. "Anything else I should know, boss?"

"You have my address. Make sure everything gets delivered today. I'll also need them to shuffle some things around when they get to the house."

"Of course," Theo says. "Whatever you need."

I help Tyler into his winter coat, hat, and gloves. Elisa hurries next door to grab her own coat, bustling to the elevator as I hit the button to go down.

"I'm surprised you didn't hire someone else to get you around the city."

She knows me too well. I hate driving in New York, but the house is in the suburbs, and I'll be heading away from the city. With Camden being sick, I usually have Theo drive me around whenever Camden is off work. I don't use a car service; I hire my own reliable men to work for me. But I put Theo in charge of the move.

"Are you mocking me?" I ask.

She holds up her hands in surrender. "I wouldn't dream of it. You do know how to drive, right?"

There she goes again, teasing me.

"Yes, I can handle it." I steal a kiss from her as we head outside into the blustery cold. Tyler's hand is latched in mine. I unlock the door and help him into the backseat, buckling him into the vehicle.

"I feel like this is goodbye," she murmurs, her brow furrowed and tight.

"You know it's not." My stomach is twisted into a ball. "Come by for dinner," I insist. "Bring clothes for work tomorrow."

I secure Tyler into his car seat and slam the door shut. The engine is running, warming the vehicle, keeping my little monster from freezing.

"You just want me to help you unpack," she says.

"You're not wrong." I lean in, my lips crushing hers in another searing kiss. "Five o'clock."

She whimpers under her breath, "You're bossy."

The smile grows on my face. "You're just now figuring that out?" Another quick kiss, and I hurry to the driver's side, watching as she hurries back into the foyer to keep warm. She waves and I climb inside the vehicle, grateful for the warmth from the heat pumping inside.

"Daddy, I miss Elisa," Tyler says.

I glance in the rearview mirror as he clutches his stuffed dinosaur and waves to Elisa.

Me too, buddy.

It feels like she's too far, too out of reach. Yes, I'll be seeing her at work and sometimes she'll come home with me, but it doesn't quite feel like enough.

But if I ask her to move in with me, won't it be too soon? I don't want to scare her away.

―――――

The afternoon blazes by with unpacking. The house is a mess. An absolute disaster. How is it that everything from storage and the condo is delivered at the same time and there's not enough space to put the furniture and boxes?

My house isn't small by any means, but I also try not to live so extraordinarily lavishly that I flaunt my money. There's no need for that. For a long time, the house was just mine and I lived alone.

Until my sister got pregnant with Tyler. We had plans for her to come stay with me, I'd help out with her son until she got comfortable raising a kid on her own. She wasn't looking forward to being a single parent in the sense that she had to do it alone.

And I wasn't going to abandon her or make her do anything on her own. We're family. We stick together.

It still hurts, walking by the bedroom where she lived for a few months, before she went into labor, and everything went wrong.

I haven't opened that door since before she died.

While I was moving out of the house and into the condo, I assigned Theo to clean out Wren's bedroom, box up her possessions and put them into storage.

Those items remain in storage, still locked away. One day, when Tyler is older, we'll go through them together. But I'm not ready and it's still too fresh a wound for me to face.

The doorbell chimes and music plays throughout the house. The movers are diligently working to unbox and put away my possessions but there's still so much to do and I hate sitting around being useless.

Theo grabs the door before I have time to get there, and I can hear Elisa's sweet voice from around the corner.

"Weston?" Her voice is like honey, and my head pops up from around the boxes as I sit on the floor, putting some of the baking sheets away.

Tyler scurries into the room, throwing his arms around Elisa. She bends down and scoops him up into her arms. "Long time no see," she says, and he drops dozens of tiny kisses to her cheek.

It's adorable and heartwarming.

In her hand, she's holding a small brown bag.

"What's that?" I ask, nodding toward the paper bag. "It's a little late for lunch." I'll be putting dinner on as soon as I find all the pots and pans. The crew already unpacked the spices, oils, and pantry essentials for me.

But the amount of work is enormous, and I don't like sitting on my ass, unless I'm helping.

"It's not lunch." She's cryptic as fuck.

I stand and embrace her in a hug. "Housewarming gift?" I guess, wagging my eyebrows at her. "You didn't have to get me anything."

She opens her mouth and closes it. "Do you give someone a housewarming gift when they've always lived here and just temporarily left?"

I shrug. "Okay, my mistake. What's in the bag?" I'm like a kid when it comes to presents and I want to know what's inside the neatly wrapped package or, in this case, the plain brown bag. It's not a liquor store type bag, so she didn't bring alcohol.

Which is fine. I have plenty of wine in the cellar.

"Fine," she says, and pushes the bag at me, rolling her eyes. There's a smirk at the corners of her lips and I watch her hand tremble as she gifts me the brown bag.

I unfold the top and glance in, confused. I pull out the empty stick, it's one of those tests that you pee on. "What is this?" The smile fades from my face. "Is this some type of sick joke?"

My stomach tenses and the room spins. "Tyler, go into the playroom." I don't want him to witness the hell I'm about to unleash on Elisa.

Has she been screwing around with other men?

She must be, in order to be pregnant.

Because I had a vasectomy. It's not possible that I'm the father.

He scampers into the playroom without asking why. Maybe he senses the tension in the air, or he just wants to go play with his toys.

Elisa shuffles her feet.

"Are you trying to pull one over on me?" I growl at her, stepping closer. I toss the test and the paper bag onto the nearby counter.

"What?" Her brow is furrowed, and her cheeks are flushed. "I'm pregnant, Weston. It's yours."

I laugh darkly, manically. She can't be serious.

"Nice try." I take a step back. The room is suffocating. It doesn't matter how big this house is, I'm suddenly claustrophobic. "Who else did you sleep with?" My eyes burn with a heated rage building inside of me.

"No one," Elisa gasps, her mouth agape. "I can't believe you, Weston. I thought you'd at least give me the time of day – not accuse me of slutting around behind your back."

I step closer, growling as I stare her down. "We haven't been together that long."

"Long enough to get pregnant! W-we weren't always careful," she stammers.

"How many other men were there?" I glance her over. She looks hurt, broken. Why? Her eyes are red, glistening with tears, but she stands her ground.

"There was only you, you numb-nuts."

I scoff at her insult. "That's real mature of you," I say.

"What makes you think you can't be the father? Because you're the only man who's fucked me in the last two years!"

Her words cut me, and I glance away.

No.

That can't be true.

"I had a vasectomy," I seethe, my hands clenched as I grip the kitchen counter to keep me steady. My heart slams into my ribcage. "It can't be mine."

"Those aren't always effective," Elisa says. "I swear, Weston, I didn't sleep with anyone else. Stop being such an ass."

Am I just supposed to believe her?

I never wanted kids.

I love Tyler, but I didn't plan for him and now this... baby. I didn't plan for that, either. My hand loosens on the counter as I fold my arms across my chest.

"It's mine?" I glance from her down to her abdomen. She isn't visibly showing yet. "How far along are you?"

"It's one hundred percent yours. Unless vibrators can suddenly make a girl pregnant." She chuckles at her joke, and I growl, stepping closer, wrapping an arm around her waist.

"You'd better throw that vibrator away," I growl at her.

"Or what?" She stares up, challenging me.

"I'm not having you vibrate our baby that you're growing." The words sound strange and foreign. *Our baby.* But I believe her, that she hasn't been with anyone else. And we haven't always been careful, because I believed the vasectomy had been effective. I wasn't worried about pregnancy and we're both clean.

I pull her tight against me, my hand in soothing circles against her back. "I'm sorry," I whisper, wishing I'd have believed her, and that the news had been happier for both of us.

"You're a grumphole," she mutters under her breath, "suggesting I slept with someone else."

"You're right." She has every reason to hate me right now, but I don't want the news to tear us apart. "I'm sorry, Elisa. I should never have said those things."

"Or thought them!"

I guide my hand to her chin, making her meet my gaze. "I'm sorry."

Her nose twitches and her bottom lip pouts as she stares up at me with wide eyes. "Apology not accepted," she says. "But you can make it up to me."

"How?" I ask, willing to do anything. I'm not a man to grovel but I said some unforgiveable things and I don't want it to tear us apart.

"I don't want to be your acquisitions assistant anymore," she says.

My stomach tenses. "You don't?" Is she quitting, again?

"I want a transfer and promotion to executive producer. And I want a pay raise now that I'll be supporting two."

I laugh under my breath and take a step back. "That's quite a change."

"I'm already doing the job. I acquire screenplays for development all the time. And we've gotten two streaming deals that have been eight figures because of my contribution. I haven't seen a cent from those deals and I'm worth every penny and then some."

"You don't have to prove your qualifications to me," I say. She's right, she's underpaid and overworked. "HR has been pushing me to hire a new Executive Producer."

She groans under her breath. "They're never going to approve me for the position."

"Doesn't matter. I'm your boss," I say. "You're not getting special treatment, you're fully qualified for the role, and frankly, you need a pay increase that won't raise eyebrows."

"And giving me the position won't turn heads?" she quips.

Did she expect me to turn down the suggestion? "Since when have you cared what others thought, Miss Emerson?"

She purses her lips. "Really, Mr. Grump? Are we doing this here, in your house?"

"Doing what?" I chide.

"Acting all business-like," she says, stepping closer. She grabs my shirt in her fist and pulls me closer. Her lips linger but she doesn't lean in the last fraction for a kiss.

"I love you," I whisper, daring to say the words aloud and hoping that it doesn't scare her off.

"It's about damn time," she says with a smirk.

I lean down, brushing her lips hungrily, pulling her tighter and closer against me.

"I love you too," she says with a huge grin. "Now, when can I move in?"

# EPILOGUE

*Elisa*

I DON'T WASTE any time when it comes to moving in with Weston. Sloane helps me do a little packing, but Weston hires the same movers, or rather, his assistant does, to handle bringing everything to his place.

At first, it feels strange, moving in with him, but we find our rhythm together, long before our little bundle enters the world.

Tyler wants a baby brother, and Weston and I will be happy with whichever we're provided. He's a doting father with Tyler and I know without a doubt he'll be great with our daughter or son.

We balance each other out. Where he tends to be overprotective with Tyler, I've come to understand his son's condition and have helped make sure that Tyler is safe while still enjoying his childhood.

He doesn't need two helicopter parents.

I struggle to get around the house, my pregnant belly protruding and making it difficult for me. When the day finally arrives and Weston rushes me to the hospital, we're overcome with joy at the little boy in our arms.

I'm lying in the hospital bed, nursing our little one, while Tyler watches from beside me, curious and attentive to his little brother.

"What's his name?" Tyler asks.

It's the one thing we've both been struggling to decide. We swore when we saw our son or daughter, we'd know.

"I want to name him Lawrence," I say, glancing at Weston. He's quiet, not rejecting the name yet. "He would be named after Wren."

Weston exhales a heavy breath and his eyes well. He glances away briefly, trying to compose himself. "That's really sweet. I like it."

"Lauren?" Tyler's nose scrunches. "That's a girl's name. It's really a boy. Right?" Tyler tries to poke his head around to see under the baby blanket.

"Yes, it's a boy," Weston says, and grabs Tyler, pulling him into his arms for tickles and cuddles.

Smiling up at the two men in my life, and now three, with the little bundle in my arms, I feel overjoyed and overwhelmed.

"Do you want to give your mom a present?" Weston whispers a little too loudly to Tyler.

Tyler spins around to face his father, and a minute later, Weston helps him down, putting the little tiger's feet on the floor.

"Will you be my mommy?" Tyler asks, bringing me a velvet box.

I gasp as Weston approaches the bed and ruffles Tyler's hair. "Good job, kid. Now it's my turn."

I clutch Lawrence in my arms as Weston falls gracefully down on one knee, his hand reaching for mine. "Elisa, we may be starting a family together, but you are my family. My life. My constant. You are as bright as the sun, and it's clear to me even in the darkest night that you are my North Star. I love you. I love our family and I want to be tied to you forever."

"You're already tied to me," I laugh, wiggling Lawrence at him.

"I want to marry you, Elisa. I want to spend the rest of my life with you. Will you marry me?"

I suck in a nervous breath, my heart pounding and the heart rate monitor growing louder, making it impossible for my nervousness to be hidden from anyone. "You had to ask me here?" I laugh, glancing at the beeping monitor as the nurse hurries into the room to check on me.

"He just proposed," I say in way of an explanation as she surveys the monitors and silences the beeping.

Her eyes widen. "And what did you say?"

"She hasn't," Weston growls at the nurse, "because you interrupted us."

There he goes again, being Mr. Grump. The poor nurse, she didn't know what she was walking into when she came barreling into the room to check on me. "It's not her fault," I defend her. "She's just doing her job."

"It sounds like you two are already married," the nurse quips with a laugh.

Weston stares, waiting for my answer.

"It's a yes, obviously!" I exclaim. How could he think otherwise?

Weston leans down, pressing his lips to mine. His fingers tangle in my hair, but he's careful of our new baby clutched against my chest.

"I want to cuddle," Tyler squeals, and climbs onto the bed, careful of Lawrence as he joins us in celebrating.

———

Thank you for reading Bachelor Grump. I hope you enjoyed Weston and Elisa's story.

**When you're a star athlete and hire a bodyguard to protect your daughter but...**

The agency sends you an adorable 5 foot 2 brunette that barely looks capable of protecting herself, let alone anyone else.

Turns out "Ryan" is Emerson Ryan, former FBI. She drop-kicks your butt to the ground to prove her point.

She's more than capable of protecting your little girl...

But you shouldn't be turned on by her fierceness.

Everyone thinks she's your daughter's nanny. She looks the part and goes along with it at your insistence until she's forced to be Bristol's babysitter. That isn't what she signed up for, and she can't protect your daughter if she's busy entertaining and cleaning up after her.

With a professional hockey career on the line, you need a nanny to help pick up the slack and maybe even a fake girlfriend.

But how long can you pretend everything is fake when the sparks are real?

This steamy hockey romance book features a grumpy single dad, a sizzling romance with plenty of drama. No cheating. HEA.

One-click Faking it with the Billionaire now!

———

And I'm thrilled to offer a sneak peek of Expose: Jaxson, a spicy slow-burn romance series.

———

*Ariella*

I ran for my life, and it was all *his* fault. Secrets had brought me over a thousand miles from home. I fled with only one thought in mind: a second chance. Starting over was my only option for survival.

I squinted through my sunglasses, shucking them to the empty passenger seat, finding it difficult to see. My vision adjusted, but the night was setting in fast as daylight fell over the horizon.

I struggled to see the narrow, snow-covered road ahead.

The streets at the bottom of the mountain had been freshly plowed and salted. The headlights on my five-speed were angled at odd intervals, casting shadows over the road covered in potholes beneath the slush.

The car jolted and bounced with my foot on the gas, splashing my scalding, stale coffee from the cup holder.

My eyes burned and welled.

"Shit!"

Tears threatened the surface, but I wouldn't cry. It wasn't the sting of blistering liquid that hurt. I'd done this to myself. I blamed him, but it was as much my fault.

Secrets surrounded my past. Benjamin Ryan had been part of those secrets, but there was more than even he knew. There were secrets I could never tell him, even as he was whisked away in handcuffs.

I packed my car with my possessions and hurried out of the state of New York. Of course, not before finding a small log cabin in the woods that I could afford in cash, sight unseen.

I also lined up a job interview at a nearby resort, but there was no guarantee of landing a position right away. My last one had ruined my life, and I couldn't even put it on my resume.

I'd have to be frugal with the few dollars left to my name, which consisted of a few ones in my wallet.

Was I bitter?

Sure as shit, but I moved on, started over, and prayed for a second chance. A fresh start is what I did, what I craved, and the only way to get that was to move.

I went back to using my maiden name: Ariella Cole. I wasn't in hiding per se. After all, I had done nothing wrong or criminal.

I couldn't say the same for him.

I didn't want to get mixed up in his illegal affairs.

I had planned on arriving at my new home before dark, but the interview had been in the afternoon at Blue Sky Resort, a ski lodge just outside of Breckenridge, Montana.

It was for a position covering other worker's shifts, everything from waitressing at the restaurant to doing housekeeping tasks and handling the ski rental equipment. I'd take whatever I could get.

The interview had seemed to go well, and they had asked to run a background check. I wasn't keen on it but I didn't have a choice, so they'd see that my ex-husband, Ben, had run up our credit. They couldn't deny me a job because of that, right?

He was serving time in federal prison for several felonies. That couldn't count against me, right?

When I'd left the resort, with my piping hot, burnt coffee, it had grown dark. The front desk attendant had given me directions since my phone died, and GPS was sketchy as to whether it worked in the mountains.

I headed for my new house, weary, tired, and worn after a lengthy interview and an even longer drive across the country. I wanted to discover my new home, climb into bed under the warm covers and sleep for a week.

The interviewer informed me they'd run my references, and I had to submit to a background check.

It sounded all good, and while I hoped the job was mine, there were no guarantees. They hadn't offered me anything yet.

I downshifted my car, but I struggled to get up the mountain.

The bald tires spun as I white-knuckled the steering wheel. The back of the vehicle fishtailed.

I downshifted again and stomped on the gas to climb the godforsaken beast of a mountain when the car slipped and slid backward downhill.

"Shit!" I screamed and stomped on the brakes hard, which only had me doing donuts as I spun and slid down the icy path of the mountain. I would have braced for impact if I had known how, but I just wanted to survive. I needed to survive.

My stomach ached with dread. My palms were sweaty, and I clung to the steering wheel, attempting to maneuver my car out of danger.

I had no control over the vehicle, like it had a mind of its own.

The car spun and smacked into a tree. The window smashed. It wasn't enough to stop the momentum from sliding down the mountain, and the back wheels skidded off the road.

By some miracle, the vehicle came to a halt. The back wheels teetered off the edge of a ravine.

The car's front appeared stable, but would it propel me downward and into oblivion if I made any sudden movements?

I glanced in the rearview mirror.

It grew darker by the minute, and I couldn't ascertain how far down the ditch went, but given the fact the entire drive up the mountain was switchbacks and dangerous, without a doubt, it was deadly.

Exhaling a soft, slow breath, I couldn't stay in the car. I needed to get help.

I hadn't seen a car on the road since I attempted to climb the damned mountain. Was there a reason for that? Did anyone live up in Breckenridge, or was I the only one crazy enough to head up there on the cusp of winter?

I probably should have traded my car in for a vehicle with all-wheel drive or a truck, but it wasn't like I could afford it.

I was strapped for cash. I spent every dime on getting to Breckenridge and paying cash for the cabin I found on one of the realtor sites online.

The place looked like a gem, backed up to a gorgeous river, and within walking distance to a few local shops in town.

This had to mean I wasn't the only one in Breckenridge, but they were smart enough not to travel at night up the mountain.

My phone was dead, and even if it had any juice left, I knew without a doubt there would be no cell service around here.

There had been no service at the bottom of the mountain. That had been when my phone still had a tiny amount of battery power.

Not that I didn't have anyone to call. My sister would expect to hear from me, but we weren't on the best speaking terms. She was pissed that I moved to Breckenridge instead of staying in New York with her.

I couldn't stay. I had to get as far away from New York and the enemies we'd made.

I glanced behind me at my knapsack. I couldn't risk reaching for it. Not until I was out of the car.

With slow precision, I unlocked the door and eased the driver's side open. I made no sudden movements.

While I'd have preferred to stay in the confines of the car that offered shelter, it teetered on the edge of a ravine. I wasn't ready to meet death.

The car creaked and groaned as I was careful to shift my weight from one foot and then the other out from the vehicle.

The vehicle didn't launch off the cliff as I had first feared. I shivered and pulled my jacket tight.

I couldn't easily open the back door from my position. The snow was several inches thick, and I had stuffed my boots in the trunk.

There was no way I could maneuver myself to grab my warm and comfy shoes. My fancy heels would have to suffice because I wasn't going barefoot. That would be even stupider in this weather.

"Okay, I can do this," I said to myself.

There wasn't another soul on the road, and I didn't even want to consider what wild animals like bears or wolves come out at night. I hadn't the slightest idea if they were nocturnal. I hoped I didn't run into any creatures because I had nothing but my hands to protect me, and well, I may as well just lie down and play dead.

Okay, so getting my bag from the backseat wasn't as easy as I thought. I exhaled a nervous breath, my stomach in knots as I climbed back into the driver's seat, reached for my knapsack in the back, along with my purse on the passenger seat.

I didn't make any sudden movements, and I backed away from the car, shut the car door, shoved my purse into the bag, and swung it over my shoulder.

My hands shook from the cold and the adrenaline coursing through my veins. I dug into my pockets, retrieving a pair of leather driving gloves. They would have to suffice.

With daylight nearly gone, I headed for the main road of the mountain.

I kept to the center of the snow-covered path. I'd probably hear something long before I'd see anything, but I wasn't holding my breath.

The moon offered the faintest bit of light to illuminate the snow-covered road.

I had no flashlight, and the darkness of night seeped in, which reminded me there wasn't a town for miles because there were no city lights nearby.

I glanced up at the heavens, the frigid night air offering way to a sparkle of stars peppering the night sky. It would be a beautiful sight if it wasn't so cold and I didn't worry about freezing to death.

My lungs hurt from the cold. With each breath inward, a thousand knives were stabbing at my lungs.

With my jacket zipped up tight, I leaned my head down toward my coat. I needed to find shelter. With sundown, the night would only grow colder.

My hands trembled even with the warmth of my gloves. The edge of the road was difficult to see with no light. It seemed even more impossible to determine if there was any evidence of shelter.

I kept walking up the mountain. The only way I could tell I was headed in the correct direction was because the wind assaulted my face, and my footprints were evidence of where I'd been.

I could no longer see my car in the distance. The broken windows may have offered little shelter from the wind, but I could have been warmer had I stayed inside the vehicle. I could also have been catapulted down the ravine had I so much as shifted the car's weight.

There was no use second-guessing my decision. I just hoped that the main road would lead off to a driveway, a house, a cabin, or some sign of civilization.

The chill of the cold brought tears to my eyes, freezing my eyelashes, stinging my cheeks. My hands were numb, and my knapsack offered no clothes. Frozen inside and out.

I stumbled over my feet.

My toes burned from the frigid air that assaulted every inch of my body. The sensation went beyond numb and tingling.

I tripped and braced myself as I hit hard-packed snow on the road, eating a mouthful. I spit out the contents as best I could.

My lips were numb, along with my cheeks.

I shivered and curled up in the fetal position in the middle of the snow-covered road. I buried my face away from the chill.

Shielding my cheeks from the cold, getting an ounce of warmth and a reprieve from the elements. I pulled my bag closer to protect me from the wind. I shut my eyes.

My body trembled, but I wasn't cold. Not like I had been earlier. Numb. Nothing but emptiness, a cold and lonely existence stabbing at me.

One-click EXPOSE: JAXSON now!

# ABOUT THE AUTHOR

Willow Fox has loved writing since she was in high school (many ages ago). Her small town romances are reflective of living in a small town in rural America.

Whether she's writing romance or sitting outside by the bonfire reading a good book, Willow loves the magic of the written word.

She dreams of being swept off her feet and hopes to do that to her readers!

Visit her website at:

https://authorwillowfox.com

# ALSO BY WILLOW FOX

Eagle Tactical Series

Expose: Jaxson

Stealth: Mason

Conceal: Lincoln

Covert: Jayden

Truce: Declan

Mafia Marriages

Secret Vow

Captive Vow

Savage Vow

Unwilling Vow

Ruthless Vow

Bratva Brothers

Brutal Boss

Wicked Boss

Possessive Boss

Obsessive Boss

Dangerous Boss

Bossy Single Dad Series

Billionaire Grump

Mountain Grump

Bachelor Grump

Ice Dragons Hockey Romance

Faking it with the Billionaire

Daring the Hockey Player

Looking for kinkier books? Try these spicy stories written under the name Allison West.

Boxsets

Academy of Littles

Western Daddies Collection

Obey Daddy Collection

The Alpha Collection

Western Daddies

Her Billionaire Daddy

Her Cowboy Daddy

Her Outlaw Daddy

Her Forbidden Daddy

Standalone Romances

The Victorian Shift

Jailed Little Jade

Prefer a sweeter romance with action and adventure?
Check out these titles under the name Ruth Silver.

Aberrant Series

Love Forbidden

Secrets Forbidden

Magic Forbidden

Escape Forbidden

Refuge Forbidden

Boxsets

Gem Apocalypse

Nightblood

Royal Reaper

Royal Deception

Standalones

Stolen Art

www.ingramcontent.com/pod-product-compliance
Lightning Source LLC
Chambersburg PA
CBHW022246020726
47496CB00004B/1095